Through the Cracks, the Shadow

Introduction – 'School for the Spectral' – Ramsey Campbell

Editor's note

'The Red Coat'	Joseph Tonge
'Inculpable?'	Alice Khoo
'The Crazed Serial Killer'	Max Mira and Aaron Checkley
'The Judgement Day'	Scarlett Quinn
'The Road'	Francesca Fonseca
'Nightmare'	Lucy Cuthbertson
'The Old Caravan'	Nathan Collings
'Shadows are Waiting'	Helen Wallwork
'The Echoing'	Will Gibson
'The Time I Watched'	Aaron Ryan
'The Butcher's Surprise'	Dylan jones
'A Desolate Street'	Sadie Cardall
'A Horror Story'	Alexander Clark
'The Queen's Escape'	Alistair Burgess
'Everything Went Black'	Ellora Chatwin
'Him'	James Turner
'Always Watching'	Sophia Campbell
'The Killer'	Jack Hertzog-Garbett
'The Phantom Monster'	Tara Odetoyinbo
'The Nightmare of Cinnamon Street'	Rishi Singh
'Practice What You Preach'	Prem Nagra
'Hermione'	Esme Mercer
'The Ghost Hour'	Kate Baker
'Cracks'	Han Khoo
'Stumbled'	Rachel Hughes
'Canned Meat'	Henry Worden-Roberts
'Corona Christmas: The Apocalypse'	Murray Cowan
'I Was Dared to'	Em Keating
'The Night That Never Happened'	Rohan Kapoor
'Watch Their Backs'	H. G. White (deceased)
'Beating Ozymandias'	Grace Klemperer
'Play with Me'	Ramsey Campbell

SCHOOL FOR THE SPECTRAL

Once again I'm honoured to be asked to introduce the Birkenhead School anthology of the macabre. Let me share my experience of the contents.

Joseph Tonge vividly evokes an ongoing tragedy of our time with an enviable eye for the eloquent image. A ghostly encounter proves more reassuring than the mundane welcome the narrator has to face. Alice Khoo uses a structure I believe Ambrose Bierce invented to triangulate the unearthly and bring it to disquieting life. Max Mira and Aaron Checkley bring off a feat I never could—collaboration, a task at which I once let Poppy Z. Brite down—and provide a twisty, indeed twisted, tale. Scarlett Quinn uses Gothic imagery to bring alive an experience we may fear awaits us all, while Frankie Fonseca traps us with an alarming shadow in a timeslip.

Lucy Cuthbertson's vignette radiates atmosphere and menace, but is it a literal nightmare? The first sentence suggests that whatever is here may recur. Nathan Collins' terse enigma preserves its mystery, as much of the best horror does. Helen Wallwork surrounds a school legend with uneasy details that insist worse is going on, and in time they congeal into outright grisliness. Will Gibson collects sensory details to build into a symphony of dread.

Aaron Ryan confronts the sort of incident that is growing all too close to everyday and the guilt it brings or ought to bring. Dylan Jones portrays a haunting as unresolved and suggestive as such incidents tend to be outside fiction. Sadie Cardall's story begins by undermining the familiar both psychologically and physically, and this is only the starting point of its relentless delirium. Alexander Clark's tale gives no quarter either, but then one defining quality of horror can be that it overtakes the underserving without reason or explanation.

Alastair Burgess's tale is thoroughly dreamlike, and unashamed of its fantasy. Ellora Chatwin wastes not a word in plunging us into gruesomeness, and the terseness of flash fiction leaves no room for relenting. James Turner reveals a secret that may lurk behind the familiar world of fashion, but we can only guess at the motives and the nature of its perpetrator. Sophia Campbell contributes a poignantly poetic contemplation of loss, and her ghost offers solace. Jack Hertzog-Garbett depicts a childlike if not childish maniac, all too convincing a creation—we may fear his equivalent is already at large. His development has been arrested but, alas, not him.

Tara Odetoyinbo's tale has all the qualities of nightmare, as inexplicable as it is inescapable. Rishi Singh needs only a page and a change of day to overwhelm Christmas with an apocalypse. Prem Nagra starts with a dream that seeps into the narrative, laying the foundation for a Faustian pact that inevitably goes awry. Esme Mercer starts quietly, even positively—a classical approach—but having brought to life a fantasy I'm sure many fans of a famously successful writer must harbour, she lets an element we took for just a background detail pounce. By contrast, Kate Baker locates her menace in A & E, escalating a panic all too everyday into grotesque terror.

Han Khoo's vision transforms before our eyes with the unpredictable mutability of dream. Rachel Hughes' cameo has the qualities of a surrealist poem. Henry Worden-Roberts' venture builds to a shuddery coda; can it have been unavoidable? Murray Cowan takes on the threat we may believe we've lived through and turns a solution into worse than the problem. Em Keating brings us a ghostly encounter that needs no substance to haunt a life; once you glimpse the beyond, you're never quite the same.

Rohan Kapoor's narrator makes that most traditional of mistakes: even if you think you're only in a fairy tale (and after all, they and the tale of terror often overlap), don't seek refuge in that house in the woods—but we're too wise, being readers, whereas we might make the same error in real life. He ends with a decidedly disconcerting claim, but then what are we to make of the equally unnerving presence of H. G. White? He appears to bring a message from a place that may be lying in wait for us, if indeed he isn't bent on sending some of us there. Grace Klemperer touches on strangeness in her first paragraph, and proceeds to weave half-glimpsed classic texts into a tale they render memorably weirder. It and others of the tales take us places only the imagination can inhabit, and that's a noble aim. Imagination is one of the treasures of the soul.

Our genial editor has kindly included a tale of mine. "Play With Me" was written for a young folks' anthology of tales of terror, but apparently fell short of requirements. Years ago Jenny (my wife) and I walked to Hilbre Island, just off West Kirby—beware the tides! During our visit I overheard a lady lying on the grass tell her child to stay by her shadow. How could I have failed to find a tale in this? I hope it's at home in this book, but that's enough of me. Here's to the future of our field and to every contributor. May they help to shape the world.

Ramsey Campbell

Wallasey, Merseyside

15 August 2022

Introduction - copyright Ramsey Campbell

Editor's note.

It is with great pleasure that we can (finally) introduce the second volume of Birkenhead School's A Ghost Story for Christmas. This book commemorates the third year of this event which is kindly supported by Ramsey Campbell. On December 1st 2021, lockdown restrictions had lifted sufficiently to allow us to enjoy an in-person event. A group of students read their own stories in the low lights of the school library to an audience of parents. Mr Campbell generously recorded a message of support to the students who were working in the tradition which he has enriched and served spectacularly through his extensive output.

The ghost story and Christmas can be associated with Dickens, via M. R. James and the BBC, although Shakespeare writes that a 'goblin story' is best for winter. My own encounter with Mr Campbell's work was a story he wrote set at Christmas in the anthology 'The Gruesome Book'. I am happy to write that students today still enjoy 'Calling Card' when I disinter it each Christmas before the end of term.

It is an honour and a privilege for the students to have the support of Mr Campbell. Not only is his critically acclaimed work compared with the greats of the genre, his initial mentor was August Derleth, who collaborated with and published the work of H. P. Lovecraft. Whilst all of sound mind would condemn Lovercraft's abhorrent misanthropic and racist views, his influence upon the genre of the Weird Tale cannot be underestimated. Ramsey Campbell can justly claim to be an integral part of the Western horror tradition and his generosity with his time, support and his own disturbing contribution to this volume, allows the students published here to boast that they have, for now, a small claim to be part of that tradition too.

I apologise for forgetting any who are deserving of thanks but I want to recognize Karl and the estates team for assisting with the facilities on the night of our event and the catering team for supplying refreshments. Also, Grace Klemperer took on the role of chief editor before the demand of examinations kicked in and I very much appreciate the editorial work carried out by: Soyra Bhagwat, Lucy Cuthbertson, John Cottier, Jake Ashcroft, Ollie Brennan, Tilly McAllister, Amelia Clawson, Amy Langan, many thanks you 'earth-treading stars'.

Unfortunately one accomplished piece was handed in anonymously and despite asking teaching staff and students no one has yet claimed it. In a morbid and facetious way, it was decided to credit Mr White, an OB and former inhabitant of Overdale whose presence still plays havoc with the technology at times.

It is now time to peer into the cracks and glimpse the shadows that wait beyond.

Mark Bell (English Teacher and event organiser)

The copyright for each text lies with its named author.

The Red Coat

Joseph Tonge

Many weeks of travelling, and it was the final stretch, the most dangerous part of the journey. The waves look fierce, the dinghy looks too fragile, and the forty other people ready to climb in have the same concerned look. The fear threatens to overwhelm me but is toned down by the excitement of getting away from the conflict and fear. We have travelled in cramped lorries and trekked through unforgiving terrain for hundreds of miles over many weeks. We have slept in filthy camps. Living our lives in the shadows.

My family have told me a new life awaits and there will be joy when we get to the UK, for it is December and Christmas is widely celebrated there. They say the UK is an accepting and peaceful country, and the people will treat us kindly. They say we will claim asylum, but I am not entirely sure what that means. Another teenager on this journey told me asylums were places where they used to lock up "crazy" people. Does that mean what we are doing is insane?

Our minder has thick skin pock-marked like a cheese grater. He made us carry the dinghy down the cliff tops to the sea. Now, as he wades knee-deep in the water, he is hissing at us in urgent tones to clamber aboard. As I step in, he squeezes my arm like he is testing fruit in the market. I know better than to complain.

I squat down next to my mother and remember stories I have heard of hundreds of people who have not survived perilous journeys like this. I recall a memory where I saw a photograph of a dead boy, a few years younger than me, lying face down on the sand where he had been washed ashore. He still wore his trainers, and his red coat was jarringly vibrant in the gruesome scene.

The minder shows two of the men how the engine works and pushes us off towards our new life. The waves come crashing over the sides. My hands soon become numb with the cold, my teeth chatter and my legs quiver with fear.

The water at the bottom of the raft becomes deeper and we frantically scoop it over the sides, the first sensations of panic starting to creep in. Suddenly, I lose my balance and fall into the murky, angry waves.

There is a dark gulp as the cold water swallows me. My efforts are useless as I sink deeper and deeper into the underwater gloom.

Hopelessly I thrash, thinking of my family and our new life, when suddenly the sea becomes impossibly clear and bright. I feel a hand grasp me. I am looking into the eyes of a boy, and he is wearing a red coat. He seems to be at one with the water, his hair trailing like an octopus' legs and his skin is luminescent. He looks at me with concern on his face and without warning pushes me hard upwards.

I shoot to the surface like a cork, coughing and spluttering. I can hear people screaming my name, and they look wild with terror, soon giving way to collapse with relief. Soaking and freezing, I am hoisted from the depths by strong hands.

I do not tell anyone what I have seen. They will surely think I have lost my mind with the fear, shock and cold. They might think I really am only fit for the asylum.

Shortly after we arrive. We have made it! People wearing official clothes are coming towards us. One sees I am soaking wet and grabs me. Before I go with him, I turn to look back at the water where the white horses are racing over the relentless tide. Dark clouds are starting to roll in but, thanks to the boy in the red coat, I no longer need to live my life in the shadows.

Inculpable?

Alice Khoo

Samira

Desperation. Terror. Suspense. But silence, and frost. The kind of emotional frost, which is invisible to the eye, but most *definitely* there. When everything stops. The heart beats faster than ever but doesn't beat at all. When everything is flaming vigorously, ablaze but chilling. The movement piqued my curiosity. I won't call for mother again. I was only embarrassed myself last time. I won't be *that girl* any longer, the name which suffering under society has given me. Well, *they* will hear that I found the creature and *valorously* fought it from my small cottage in the village. The creature was gone though. But I *saw* it emerge into the shadows. I am certain. I have been traumatized by this terrible, grotesque, freaky being in my own bedroom for a month almost now. I barely ever see it, once or twice a week I suppose. This is my chance to prove it exists. I won't deny, I'm not ready. Everything inside vibrates, but I must prove this to myself now. Leg extended. 'MOTHEERR!' I wasn't thinking now. How could I? I could only scream. Every cell told me to get out. I obeyed with only a split-second hesitation. The corridor was cold, chilling. The door slammed against the wall crashing, sending rippling bangs through the house. Mother was gone though. 'M-M-OTHER?' no. no. Gone. Down with hope. With Faith. Everything I know. Desperation…terror… regret…

Jessica

Samira, *Ew*. Screaming in the corridor, ugh. Probably some dumb fantasy about 'black shapes that move blah-blah', I clutched my night gown and strutted through the corridor. 'Samira?' no reply? – *rude*. She advanced towards me. Huh. Kind of creepy, but not enough to scare me. 'Samira I'm going out tomorrow I need *sleep*' still no reply? 'Samira! Why are you so close?' Her eyes blazed with hostility that I had never seen before. A jagged throb. The last thoughts I thought.

Helena- Mother

Jessica? Jessica! Uncertainty I was not born to cope with. No breaths. 'No!' Not ever. Jessica was dead. Never again, Ever, will she go shopping, or eat her favorite foods, or even *breath*. Wound up in my own sense of loss, I didn't stop to question how she died. Bent over her, my hands on her heart, I just sobbed. Dust particles floated around me. I can't even care. But I could. I saw the face of my lost daughter in these phantom shapes. Blinking vigorously, surely just bereaved, I stared. Her full figure formed. 'Jessica!' I whispered, the phantom girl wore a night gown and strutted down the corridor.

'Samira?' the phantom girl said, I was surprised how irritated she sounded. I then turned around. There, standing in the corridor, was a translucent phantom *Samira*. The scene frightened me, but inside I was burning with curiosity. 'Samira I'm going out tomorrow I need *sleep*' Her tone, again shocked me, it was petty and pampered. 'Samira! Why are you so close?' Samira indeed had been slowly plodding down the corridor. *Strange*. Samira's eyes abruptly lit with fury, passion, strong passion, I could tell. She pushed her hand against Jessica's chest. Expression unchanged. Great, black, thick vines tightened around Jessica. The phantom lolled to the floor. To the same place the corpse was lying. The phantoms evaporated. And I ran out of there stuck in horror. I've lost Jessica, but I've lost Samira too. I cared for her, but never let her know. She was only a foster after all. In that moment, I felt all of Samira's passion, all of her hatred, all of her strength. I felt like a true mother.

The Crazed Serial Killer

Aaron and Max

A man was lying in bed one evening when he noticed there were lots of sirens on the streets outside. And there was a helicopter flying around overhead, and the sounds of barking dogs and shouting people. He looked out his window and saw a great deal of police activity, so he went online to discover what was going on.

"Serial Killer Escapes!" said the headlines. As he read further, the man discovered a crazed killer had broken loose and that he was believed to be in the man's neighbourhood. But he wasn't too worried. As the night wore on, the noise wound down, and the man went to bed.

Suddenly, the man was startled awake. He thought he had heard a sound. He listened carefully and was just about to go back to sleep when he heard it again. This time he was sure someone was trying to get in his front door. The man looked down the hallway, terrified, not knowing what to do. The only way out of his room, without going into the hallway, was through the window. He couldn't climb out. Could he? His mind was made up as he saw the door wobble in its frame as someone threw their entire weight against it.

Without another moment of hesitation, the man leapt out of his window and ran into his yard. He paused to look over his shoulder, just in time to see the light go on in his bedroom and a team of police officers pile in. before he jumped out of the window, the police had already circled around the house, to try and catch him off guard, without him knowing.

The man had escaped prison several times before but weirdly he has always come back to the same house, like he needs something from that house that he wants to hide from the police.

The police and FBI were still trying to find out why the criminal went to the same house every time. It came top the moment when they were going to search the house that the criminal went to. Before we went there, we interviewed the criminal and he said, "the reason that I go to the same house every time, I need it back or I'll get it back myself".

Then, we asked him what he wanted the answer we got is my mum and dad. The police were shocked with this answer it was time to search the house. What they found was shocking and they started to worry.

The Judgement Day

Scarlett Quinn

Silence. Darkness. Solitude. Or so I thought. It depends on your point of view; it depends on what you believe in. If you refuse to believe in ghosts, then I am alone in this place or maybe not even here at all. On the contrary, if you do believe in them, then I'm surrounded on each side. A crowd made up not of human beings, but a multitude of presences enclosing around me. They are just like me. I am neither in the land of the living nor the land of the dead. I'm a ghost in the Halfway Place waiting to have my fate decided. My life, if it's even considered a life anymore, is not in my hands. All I have to do is pass the test, to see if I tip the scales of the Judgement to the side of overall good. If you are judged to be evil, you have an eternity of suffering and misery to expect. However, it's nothing like how Hell is talked about on Earth, it's worse.

We are left to wallow in anxious uncertainty in the Halfway Room. Everywhere is bleak. The air is thick with must. Dust coats the gothic windows; cobwebs reach to greet each other across the corners of the room. Outside a layer of fog engulfs the rolling hills and the sky is a stormy ocean with crashing waves of clouds and rain, occasionally set alight by brilliant lightning bolts. The floor is a canvas of cracked grey stone, rotting wooden beams decorate the high ceiling and the menacing mahogany desk is positioned at the end of the room. In its drawers holds records of every action, every movement, every breath I have taken in my life, all to hindrance the outcome of my Judgement.

The wait is unbearable. My heart pounds, threatening to tear out of my chest. My knuckles crack as I grip onto my chair, holding on for dear life. Not wanting to let go, not wanting to face my fate. I frantically wrack my brain, trying to recall the life that I had lived. I had lived a good life; I had been a good person. I think. Surely, I would be judged to be good. Wouldn't I? I look around me, everyone looks the same, heads drooped down to the floor, frail figures loosely clinging on their bones, lifeless eyes sunken into the ocean of their skulls. Eyes that have witnessed everything, including death.

It feels like I have been here for years, yet it has only been minutes. Just when I feel my sanity slipping away, my name is called. The moment that I have been dreading. I am about to find out what lies in wait for me for the rest of eternity. Whether I will go to Heaven or to Hell. Violently shaking, I manage to push myself up out of my seat, beginning the dreaded walk towards the grand oak doors at the end of the room. Each step I take, my body weighs down heavier until I feel as if I am dragging myself along the floor, unable to take any more. Trickles of sweat slip down my face as I approach the Desk of Judgement. I turn to the receptionist, confirm my name, and are placed in the Judgement seat, all in one swift movement. This was it. The end of the beginning, with a new chapter about to be opened. A chapter that could go any of two ways, and I pray with all my being, that it is going to have a good ending.

"One of the doors will open depending on how you have been judged." The receptionist calls out, but they sound so far away that I don't hear the rest of their instructions.

"Commence the Judgement!"

My life flashes before my eyes as one of the towering doors drag open with a skull-splitting creak. Hours seem to pass by until the door hits the wall with a deep groan. I peer into the room that lies beyond the gateway, a tsunami of horror washing over me as I see smoke rising above the crumbling crimson steps descending into a blazing inferno. A scene that resembles the fiery pits of Hell.

This can't be happening; something has gone wrong. There must have been an error in the Judgement. This can't be right. Surely this can't be the way I'm going to have to endure the rest of my existence.

Before I can do anything, I feel a formidable force drag me towards the sweltering pit, voices echoing around my body.

"Your Judgement has been made. You have been judged to be evil, and you will now begin your descent into Hell."

The Road

Frankie Fonseca

The road was long and winding, a dead end with one way in and one way out. The houses on the road dated back to the early 19th century, with a rich history of intrigue and mystery. The large beastly trees arched over the dimly lit streetlamps, touching in the middle of the wide carriageway.

Lucy was meandering down her road. Not really focused on anything. She was walking slowly, half on the pavement half on the road dragging her feet.

Then suddenly something caught her attention. She wasn't quite sure what, but the road was a little bit darker and a little bit colder than it was before, even the wind was picking up. Her surroundings looked weird. And then she realised it, the once electric street lights had turned into gas lights, the large TV screen of number 26 had turned into a book shelf with a flickering candle stick on it. She even thought that she heard the sound of a horse and carriage in the distance.

What was happening? She sensed someone or something behind her.

She stopped slowly and turned her head then her whole body. She strained her eyes in the half-light but could see nothing, nobody. She still felt someone watching her, following her, chasing her, but there was no one there nothing more than a shadow. And then she realised the thing that had been bugging her all along the shadow she saw wasn`t her own. Lucy began to run as fast as she could.

Each house she passed by was in darkness. There were no lights on and seemingly no one at home. Lucy felt very much alone but she wasn't alone. There was movement and audible whispers coming from the left and the right. More and more shadows appearing by the second. Her house was almost within reach and soon she'd be home, soon she would be safe. But Lucy never arrived home. She never arrived back. She disappeared like so many others on that road over the years, never to be seen again...

Nightmare

Lucy Cuthbertson

I take the same route as always, at the same time as always. With a bunch of flowers clutched in one gloved hand and my phone in the other, the bitter November air stings my face as I walk, forcing me to retreat further into my thick woollen scarf. My headphones quietly drown out my thoughts and the sound of damp, stale leaves rustling underfoot. We are on the brink of dusk and the edge of winter, and this seems to have compelled every other person to stay inside. The sun has not disappeared completely but enough that the orange street lamps are dimly casting their warm glow. The light is not quite strong enough to stretch all the way to the subsequent one and so I walk along- being plunged into blackness and shadows every so often- the trees like hands reaching out to me.

By the time I reach the stone arch signifying the entrance, etched with the words 'Est. 1666', darkness drenches me. I slowly push the iron gates further open, the creak of the rusting iron echoing around the walls as they groan into action, and without the regular lamps illuminating the path, the only source is a sliver escaping the door of the time-worn church and a singular lantern that seems to be fading. Ivy snakes up the bricks of the church, leaking from and filling every crevice. Now that it is getting late, the chill is burning my skin and the wind has picked up, leaves dancing and swirling about my feet.

The breeze brushes past me, tickling my exposed skin; it is getting louder, too, like shallow, quickening breaths down my neck. Despite the graveyard being devoid of life, the winding path is muddied with tracks of footprints and markings. I hear the noise of feet- light on the ground and in abundance. I am paralysed with panic, frozen. I spin around, searching for some rationality. The only noise is the sound of my own heartbeat, drumming and drowning the wind, and the leaves, and the sound of darkness. A shadow darts like a blink in my periphery. I turn to see a rat scurrying along the wall above me, looking at me with the same panic that I feel. I laugh audibly with relief, and when I do so, I feel heard. There is an overwhelming feeling of a breach of my privacy, a sense of someone hearing something they weren't supposed to.

As I round the corner past the church, my stomach drops and in an instant, I can't feel the cold anymore. My eyes dart from the path to the bushes to back where I have just walked as my mind is trying to process what I am seeing. Panic rises up my body and bubbles up my throat in the form of a scream. Through an instinct that I didn't realise I had, my hand clutches my mouth, forcing me to swallow my scream. I look down and at a glance, there are mounds upon mounds of soil ahead of me. Broken slabs of stone lie strewn across the path, painted in soil and dirt.

My eyes slowly creep upwards and overwhelming dread paralyses me. I am in a nightmare; as I turn to run, my feet stay firmly planted to the floor. My head feels so light that I can't think and my limbs feel so heavy that the idea of running seems impossible. As I look up, the scream that I previously buried, escapes me and echoes, bouncing off every corner, like a shard of glass that is ripping through the air. I am met with a wall of figures, shadows, shapes that are staggering, crawling, dragging towards me. I spin round, only to be faced with limbs, reaching out of the soil, fingers clawing. Their skin is taut and almost transparent, stretched across their bones and disintegrating. Their faces are withering away, rotting cases of what they were- their veins beneath are blackened and shrivelled. Gasps for breath as they stretch out their decaying hands and I see their ribs expand as the cold air flows into them. They seem to multiply, constructing an army that seems to be advancing with every deafening thud of my heartbeat.

Their staggers are slow but purposeful, angered. Their decaying limbs are outstretched in desperation and sunken, pale sockets bore into me thirstily. As they near me, I can see skin that has worn away in places, been gnawed at. Their bones are gnarled and crooked, crawling with worms that engulf. I sink to the ground, pressing my eyes tightly shut. I scream a scream that empties my being but when I look upwards for someone, for something, all I can see is looming figures and fingers that wrap themselves around my hands, my legs, my arms, my feet, my neck. All I can feel are thousands of shallow breaths trickling down my neck and all I can do is pray that I will wake up.

The Old Caravan

Nathan Collins

Darkness grew like oil seeping from an unknown source. The floorboards creaked after every step and with that came the throbbing in my legs. My eyes closed, trapped in a vortex to hell. Trapped in a vortex into oblivion.

My legs feel numb as an inscrutable surge of pain flooded through me. I collapsed on the floor, the room spinning. Blood trickled down the side of my hand. The room seemed tto spin faster until it was agonising vision of what I had stepped into. I couldn't distract myself from this; the blood only seemed to get thicker. My will to exist was fading.

A light emerged from the darkness of my mind; it seemed to grow bigger until it was an eerie image stuck in my head.

The old caravan.

Blood continued to ooze down the walls seeming to capture me in a fruitless home. The landscape was barren it was only my thoughts haunting me now. My body lay lifeless on the floor. I was aware still. There was a presence around me.

The walls shook vigorously and my face was slumped into a forlorn death grimace.

Nothing now remained. Only the caravan.

Shadows are Waiting

Helen Wallwork

She ran. Ran down through the forest, not daring to look back. She flung the door open, and looked in horror as realisation dawned on her. She knew it was too late, and turned around to accept her fate.

"It is 7:00am, please wake up. It is 7:00am, please wake up..." The alarm repeated. I groaned, and rolled out of bed. I looked across the room to see that Dara was already awake and ready. Not surprising for a teachers' pet like her. I looked in the mirror, seeing my droopy eyes, with big dark circles under them. I noticed Amelie, in the bunk above me, hadn't come down yet. Amelie was my best friend, and she wasn't a morning person. However something felt off, as usually she would have at least complained about getting up. After getting changed, long after Dara and Charlotte had left for breakfast, I hurriedly clambered up the ladder, to wake her up.

"Hey, idiot." I whispered. She didn't respond, so I shook her.

"Amelie!" I said, louder this time in case she couldn't hear me. With paranoia, I noticed that I couldn't see the rise and fall of her chest as she breathed, and her back was turned to me, which worried me even more. My heart raced, as my head swarmed with possibilities. Nervously, I reached out to her to roll her over, drag her out of bed if I needed to. As I grabbed her waist, I noticed something. Her skin didn't feel right. It was cold, but also it didn't feel like skin. It felt like fabric that had been stretched around a... pillow? I pinched it, and I felt the polyester stuffing. I drew my hand back, and took off the sheet. Underneath was a pillow that had written on it: *'ENJOY YOUR BREAKFAST, FILLE CRÉDULE'* in block capital letters. I jumped off the ladder, and checked the time. 7:30; I had missed breakfast. I growled in frustration. As three girls re-entered the dormitory, I stared, scowling at the dark-haired french girl in front of me. I threw the closest thing I could grab at this 5'7 monster. Which she caught, naturally.

"*Mon dieu*, you get very angry when you don't eat. Anyway you should be glad that you missed breakfast. There was a big assembly about some stupid myth that this old-fashioned school still believes in. Something about salt and a monster. What is it, *un escargot*? How scary. It's silly, *non?*"

I agreed- a myth about a snail monster? Sounded dumb. I looked at the object in her hand. It was… a dagger? With the sheath on, thank goodness, but I was still confused. Nobody owned a dagger in this dorm, not that I was aware of, anyway. I noticed that she was also looking at it.

"Is this yours?" She asked, apparently thinking what I was.

"No, it's not yours?" I was puzzled. There was no way Dara or Charlotte owned a dagger.

"No." She shook her head. "That is odd." Anyway, we should probably go, first period starting soon."

"Good point. What do you have first?" I asked, my mind still focused on the mystery dagger, which had now been placed on my bed.

"French, *trop facile*. You?"

"Study skills." I sighed. I had dyslexia, which meant that I could drop languages in school. It did mean that I had to do study skills though, during the periods that I would have had languages in. Normally, I wouldn't mind study skills, but since the unexplained disappearance of Miss Lyte, I had Ms Manson as a cover teacher. Ms Manson was the school librarian, and she was horrible. She never let me ask questions, and I'm convinced she loathed me, as her obsession with reading clashed with my "inability to read". It wasn't that I couldn't read, it was that I struggled to read. I sloppily made my way to the library, noticing a poster on the noticeboard as I did so. It appeared to be about the snail-monster myth that Amelie told me about.

'BE WARNED:

SHADOWS ARE WAITING FOR YOU THIS WINTER

Hi all,

For those who are staying with us over the winter holiday, please remain extremely alert. 100 years ago, this school was cursed. A student who attended this school was reported missing on Thursday the 16th of December, 1920. This naturally caused a panic among students, as many who were close to her had spoken to her the night before the disappearance. A group of students brought it upon themselves to look for her, and left a note in their dormitory that was signed by all of them, so the school knew that they hadn't been kidnapped or similar, and that this was of their own free will. The next morning, Friday 17th, this note was found. As the students had not returned, police were called and search parties were sent out. The students were found in the surrounding forest, their hands tied above their heads, attached to trees in a circle formation, with the missing student's dead body embalmed and holding a rolled up note, which read; '5/10, see you in a century.' The cause and time of death could not be identified for any of the bodies.

It has been 100 years since that day…'

I stopped reading. I let out a breath that I didn't know I had been holding. That story was horrifying. And to think that it could happen today, or tomorrow, or the day after that… Something caught my eye. At the bottom of the poster, in bright red letters, it read:

'SPIRITUAL PROFESSIONALS AND POLICE ARE ARRIVING ON SATURDAY 19TH. THEY RECOMMEND TO LEAVE SALT WATER IN A BOWL NEAR EVERY ENTRANCE, INCLUDING DOOR, WINDOW, AND VENTILATOR. STAY SAFE.'

I heard footsteps. I froze in fear.

"You can read all that nonsense but you can't read a simple children's book?" A horrible grating voice called out to me. I exhaled. It was just mean old Ms Manson.

"I can read a children's book!" I protested, turning around to face her. "I just-" I stopped. Ms Manson looked… off. After months of seeing the same old wrinkly face, this caught me off guard. Usually, her eyebrows were furrowed. Her lips were tight, and pressed into a snarl. Her eyes were cold and cruel. Her chin was pointed up, and her breath smelled of rotten rat corpses. Now, while her breath still stank, her eyebrows were ever so slightly downturned at the corners. Her lips were loose, and simply seemed sad. Her eyes were anxious. It felt wrong. There was definitely a problem.

There was something wrong with today. As I sat in French class, I could tell. Maybe it was the witch ancestors in my head, but I couldn't help staying on edge. Every little movement, every little sound. After French, I walked to religious studies, staying alert. Passing the library, I noticed Alex, a girl in my dorm. She was the school's worst student. Rumour had it that she only stayed in the school because her parents didn't want her back, but I didn't trust rumours. She had short brown wavy hair that only reached her ears, with a red ombre effect at the bottom. Her eyes were a very vibrant shade of brown, and she always had a piercing glare that screamed: "Don't talk to me." Physically speaking, she was very small, although slightly muscular in the shoulders. On weekends, when we went to town, she lazily wore baggy trousers with oversized t-shirts on warm days, and oversized hoodies on colder days. Not right now though. She was currently wearing the school uniform- she preferred trousers over skirts. Her tie was surprisingly neat- I believed it was because of the amount of times she had been told off. Her shoes had been scuffed on multiple occasions, and her socks had fallen down. I would never be caught looking like that. I do admit though, it was pretty adorable- like a pageant puppy who had rolled in mud.

During this train of thought, I was distracted by staring at her, and bumped into Amelie, Alex's best friend, who I also shared a dorm with.

"Oh my gosh, I'm so sorry!" I squeaked apologetically. She narrowed her eyes at me and muttered, with her light French accent: "Be more careful." I had a feeling she wasn't referring to me bumping into her.

Awkwardly we walked together, keeping our distance. Amelie was tall and intimidating, she wasn't someone I wanted to cross. I didn't want to cross anyone really, but Amelie seemed like she had power over me. Not in a way that she'd kill or torture me, goodness no. But I had a feeling she could ruin my life. Badly.

At break time, I went to the library to study, and realised there was another detention being held there. I held my breath and attempted to avoid eye contact, as Alex and Amelie were there. I sat down at a desk and got a textbook out, and began taking notes. Although our exams had finished a month ago, it felt wrong to take a break from learning, and I was determined to continue to revise for the whole holiday. I sighed; this would be a long winter.

I sat in the library with Amelie; we were serving detention together. Prissy Dara entered again, definitely to study more. I groaned. We were stuck in the library all break and she chose, of her own free will, to study? She was crazy. Surely she wasn't going to spend her whole holiday revising. What a waste.

"Alexandra, focus. Don't make me keep you in here at lunch time to finish this work." Ms Manson snapped. I noticed I had been staring at Dara for a while. Amelie nudged me. I looked at her, and she looked hurt. I was confused. Why would she be hurt? Did I do something? She signed something to me; we had been learning British sign language to communicate in class or detention when the teacher wasn't looking.

'Why were you looking at her?'

'I wasn't, promise. Daydreaming.' I signed back.

'Fine. Do the work, I'm not missing lunch.' She turned back to her work. She had a point. It was Friday today. That meant hotdogs. And hotdogs sell out really fast. I tapped Amelie on the shoulder.

'Copy?' I signed. She sighed and showed me her paper. I scrawled down what Amelie had written, then we both went up to Ms Manson and handed our work in. As I followed Amelie out, Ms Manson grabbed my backpack.

"What the-" I started. Ms Manson covered my mouth with her hand, and indicated to me to be quiet. She handed me a note and said: "Don't tell anyone."

I packed up to leave the library, as break was coming to an end, and the bell was about to ring. As I did so, I noticed Ms Manson with her index finger on her lips, handing Alex a note and whispering to her. I felt a small surge of jealousy; why was Alex being treated specially? Why not me? What more did I have to do to gain the attention of the teachers? But it washed over. Alex was a troublemaker, of course she needed special attention. She couldn't just get away with everything. However, my hairs were tingling, and I couldn't look away. Ms Manson put her left hand on Alex's shoulder, before she left- and a small cloud of lilac smoke evaporated rapidly into the air. Something was wrong. This was wrong. I immediately took my bag and walked towards the door, unnaturally fast and robotically. I passed Ms

Manson and quickly inspected her left hand. There was a ring on her middle finger, and I could sense dark magic in it. I marched quickly, attempting to find Alex. Fortunately, I could trace her, with the smell of dark magic so strong and identifiable. I quickly attempted to get to her, among the crowd of people, but then I sensed it again. I turned quickly and saw another student exiting the library. I panicked, and then I noticed yet another student, who had been quite possibly cursed, entering the building. The smell was so strong and suffocating that I shoved my way outside, to try and breathe normally. I had no idea what was happening. I passed another student who smelt this way, and their shoulder bumped into mine. I felt a painful shock where contact was made, and noticed that the student had some sort of symbol branded on their shoulder.

My shoulder felt hot. I put my hand on it and ran to my next lesson, history. Ms Manson must have had really hot hands. History was my third favourite subject, after Art and Geography. I found it so fascinating that we could learn all this information about civilization from thousands of years ago! I didn't like the writing part though. This history lesson was special though. For the past week we had been learning about the history of this school, and if I was correct, that meant today we would learn about the "curse". On the poster, it mentioned a curse, but it didn't really say anything about it. I was really looking forward to today's lesson. A short while later, when the class had settled down, the one hour period began.

We learnt about the curse, although not as much as I would have liked. It was briefly mentioned: "The headmistress' daughter, who was a student at the time angered these unknown spirits, by picking ten sacred flowers from their lands. She was the student who went missing first. Rumour has it her soul was taken in exchange for the flowers, however in history we don't rely on rumours…"

From this and the poster I saw earlier, I concluded that they were taking a soul in exchange for each flower taken. Which meant five girls would be robbed of their souls this year. But if today was the last day of school… either it would be today or during the holidays. And if it was during the holidays then I was doomed. There were only about ten people staying for the holidays, including me. So there was a 50% chance I would be taken. Oh no.

I headed to my dorm by the nurse's orders. I lay on my bed, and a feeling of depression washed over me. Something was going to happen to these girls. Including Alex… Someone walked in. It was Amelie. I could sense powerful magic flowing in her veins, which I had never sensed before. She turned to me, and her eyes had changed. Her normally white sclerae were black, and her irises were red. Her pupils weren't visible, and she stared at me, menacingly. She approached me, and I backed away, in fear. She opened her mouth, and her canines seemed sharper and bigger than usual. She spoke: "Protect Alex when I'm gone. She is in extreme danger." Then she left.

Finally, the end of the day. I was so glad. It would be the holidays tomorrow! I grinned, walking back to my dorm. Lazily, I threw my blazer onto my bed. The note that Ms Manson had given me earlier fell out of my pocket. Quickly, I grabbed it, hoping no one had seen it. I may not like Ms Manson, but something felt different about her today, so I decided to give her a chance. I turned the note over, to see what it said, but as I did, Dara started coughing and wheezing, as though she was having an asthma attack. Immediately I turned to her, and moved closer to help, but she held her hand up, in a "stop" gesture. Her fingertips had turned slightly blue, and I felt horrible not helping her, but I decided to respect her wishes as Charlotte seemed to know what to do, and turned back to the note. I jumped on my bed, and looked at the note. "Meet me in the library, just after dinner." it read. The writing was messy, and seemed to glint red although there was no red light in the room.

"What is that, Alex?" A voice called out. It was Amelie. I flinched and hit my head on the bottom of the top bunk. Whilst I was being clumsy, Amelie tried to yank the note out of my hand, but in my panic, I still held tightly onto the bottom of the note. The note ripped, and I was left with "just after dinner" and slightly more than half of the words on the top left diagonal. I looked up at Amelie, and she seemed upset. She dropped the paper on the floor, and left the room.

"Amelie, where are you going?" I tried asking her, but she had gone too far away to answer me. I figured it was best not to follow her.

I watched as Alex and Amelie tore a note that Alex had been holding apart. my vision was blurred so I could not see what was written on the note, but I saw red ink- at least I thought it was ink- glimmering on the paper. But after it tore in two, I felt slightly better- my vision gradually unblurred- and could no longer see red ink on the two shreds that each person was holding. Alex looked exasperated, and Amelie wore a look of hurt and betrayal. Amelie left the room again, and to be frank, I didn't notice her re-enter after she left before.

A sudden thud and crunching of leaves startled me. A dark figure started to emerge from behind the pine tree...

It was Dara! She had showed up. But this was bad, right? We were all about to have our souls ripped out of our body and hung, just like those students from 100 years ago. She would just be an extra soul they would take. It made me question why they even wanted our souls, but I had no time to think about that. She brandished a dual-sided sword, holding it like a master. The monster's five eyes turned to look at her, one by one. Its mouth seemed to grin, although it was hard to tell, with its gunk dripping everywhere.

Light rain started falling, and the monster simply absorbed it and grew. Dara's blade cowered, and she looked incredibly insignificant from a distance. The other girls had started to run, and as bad as I felt for Dara, risking herself for us, I seized the opportunity and ran. I had only ran for a short while, until I heard a blood-curdling scream. I turned around and saw Dara, limp next to a tree. her head was bleeding and the sword had pinned her shirt to the tree, meaning she couldn't move. The monster seemed to be still, and I couldn't bear seeing her in pain and useless. I unsheathed the dagger, and headed towards Dara. I briefly looked at the other girls, who shook their heads at me and stood, frozen in fear.

I reached Dara, hastily cutting the part of her shirt that had been pinned. The sword was impaled too deep in the tree to salvage, so I had to leave it there. The rain got heavier, and the moon started to appear. My hair stuck to my face caused by a combination of sweat and rain. I heard a horrible squelching noise that scared me into staring.

It no longer had five eyes. Where the five hollows had been, there was now one giant eye, totalling six eyes. I had no time to question how this happened, as its terrible eyes looked in the direction of the school. It slowly progressed to the school.

Was now the time to play the selfless hero, to save everyone at school? I charged towards it, yelling, holding the dagger above my head. As I neared, I noticed how disgusting it smelt. It smelt like puke after eating too much cake, it smelt like feces that belonged to a cow with diarrhea, it smelt like the compost bin before it was emptied, it smelt like a used nappy that had been deposited in the wrong bin. It made me gag, and my eyes teared up at the bottom. Suddenly, I didn't have the courage. As I looked at this ten foot tall brown, monster dripping with lumps of semi-congealed slime, I gulped and thought to myself: 'What am I meant to do? A small dagger like this can't do anything.'

Slowly, it moved towards me. It looked at me with its hollow eyes. I backed away, nervously. Its hand raised in the air and it tilted its head, if you could even call it that. I dropped the dagger in fright. I stared up as the fluid on its hand started to drip off, revealing its terrible claws. I took a few steps backwards slowly, as I caught on to its intentions, then I ran. I felt a powerful gust of wind and heard my shirt get torn- then I fell.

I tumbled to the bottom of the hill. I noticed I had cuts and scratches nearly everywhere. I felt a sensation of chills down my back as I realised; we had gotten split up. The four other girls- they weren't with me. I tried calling out to them, but my voice came out as a croak. I heard a big grunt, followed by a series of short breaths, and turned around to see Dara, who had so selflessly showed up to save us.

I noticed she had a deep scratch on her stomach. It was nearly the full width of her abdomen- right underneath her diaphragm- and was bleeding heavily. I panicked, and frantically yanked my tie off, to help stifle the flow. Breathing heavily, I noticed I could make out the school observatory tower, which was located directly in the middle of the campus, and faced the main gate. I could see the left side of the tower, meaning I would have to head right in order to get to the gate. Or I could go left, and find the side entrance and try to squeeze both of us through. It was closer, and I was desperate. Hoisting her up on my shoulders, feeling her warmth ever so slowly drain, I stood up. I faced towards the side gate, and ran.

I could hear small whimpers of pain from her, when I took sharp-ish turns because of the trees, but they were drowned out by the rushing if the wind past my ears as I ran, my own heavy breathing, and my pulse which had increased significantly since this morning.

I ran, holding her bent over my shoulder. We came to a clearing, the school's observatory tantalisingly close. I stopped, sitting down to catch my breath. I adjusted her so that she was laying on my lap, and hoped it was more comfortable. I wasn't going to put her on the floor, not with the still-wet mud and her injuries. She was still breathing, shakily though. I took the opportunity to check how well my tie was covering her wound- but it had come undone. Her stomach had been bleeding, and I had no idea how long it had been. I tried to find something to substitute, but nothing would work without one of us getting hypothermia. I would've been glad to use my shirt, but I was our only way back, considering how badly she could have hurt her legs. There was nothing I could do.

She lay there in my arms, bleeding, staring at me soullessly, my hand keeping her head upright. She lifted up her hand and signed something.

'I love you.'

And I felt guilty that I had not said the same.

The Echoing

Will Gibson

The noise of brisk walking echoed through the empty halls of the basement floor, the only noise you could hear apart from the faint noise of cars above me. I walked through a long dimly lit corridor, the walls plastered with pipes. The only light source was from small bulbs that cast a radius of only; as each light was placed fifteen feet apart from each other, there was five feet were I walked through an empty void.

I was slowly making my way to the end of the corridor were a brightly lit set of elevator doors which led to 73 floors of the rest of the building and the only way out of the basement. As I walked through the rest of the corridor, going in and out of the light, I heard noises coming from the empty hall ways. A susurration from the pipes hissed in the background; each time I walked out of the light it seemed another pipe threatened to burst. As I got closer to the elevator the noises quietened into a background static. I started to hear more noise now but this time it was faint walking, echoing my steps, but heavier.

The elevator got closer. The steps behind me quickened the closer to the elevator I got and by the time I had reached the metallic doors, they were at full sprint. I stepped into the warm embrace of the deep, orange glow of the elevator light. I looked at the panel of 73 numbers I pressed the nearest one. I stood glaring at the electric sign noting what floor the elevator is currently on; it read floor 'B'.

The elevator rang its arrival at each floor, opened its doors and then continued its ascent.

The symphony of hissing pipes had been replaced by the 'ding' of each floor and the swipe of the doors. I stared into the pattern of endless lights and void. 'Ding', dark then light. Ding, dark, light. Ding, dark, light.

A small movement in the dark me look closer into the patches of void, the void stared back at me.

Ding. Dark.

I saw something at the end of the tunnel, someone was there.

Ding. Dark. Light.

I looked at this person again. Were they on every floor? Were we even moving? A low pitched popping sounded at random intervals, filling my ears and head, engulfing any previous thoughts. I could hear nothing and everything at the same time. The temperature of the tunnel was slowly rising, my face must have turned a dark shade of red and sweat dripped from my face and down the back of my neck.

I turned around staring blankly at the elevator. We were at floor 28. Only another few minutes.

I breathed in and out. I must have been hallucinating from the gas leaking out of the pipes.

Ding.
Dark.
Light.

The man had come closer. I could – ding - make out his silhouette – ding - he was taller than the ceiling, he also had some sort of large, bladed weapon.

Light.

I stared now into a face; it was a peculiarly indistinguishable shape, it was dizzying, the dimensions of the shape were changing each part of its face folding in on itself endlessly. I checked back on the floor numbers - nothing - an empty void, a window into nothing.

I looked back at the apparition, its axe held high above its head swinging down, opening more and more pipes, tearing them like they were nothing. I slumped against the doors. I had given up there is just no point anymore. I looked back at the person leaving, walking through that hall, in and out of light and all that was left was the sound of brisk walking echoing through the hallway.

The Time I Watched

Aaron Ryan

It was a lovely autumn afternoon; misty and cold with a hint of frost. When everything seemed well, like nothing could ever go wrong. A weak sun was shining and the children played with the leaves in the park. I stopped at the lake for a picnic, where the frost had started to melt. I could have stayed there forever. By the time I finished, it was dark. It was time to go home and I had to walk through the city. On my way back, I heard shouts as loud as a fog horn. The cries of desperation continued.

"Help me! Help me!" He was now screaming.

I turned the corner, only to see two police officers abusing a black man. The man looked at me, straight in the eye and cried for help. The evening mist blocked my view from the officers. Suddenly I heard a gunshot and it all went silent.

I ran, never looking behind me because I did not want to see what I thought had happened. I went to bed early without eating and just contemplated my options.

"Do I tell the police, or will it be easier to just leave it?"
"Maybe it was just a warning shot?"

I was not sure. In the morning, when I turned on the TV, I learned what I wished had not happened. I saw on a news report that a man had been shot, and they thought it was because of his race. I knew I had messed up big time! I sat down.
"I mean, I need to tell the police," I thought.

My hands were shaking so much one could think there was an earthquake. I picked up the phone to call someone but then I thought I could get charged for it. And not reporting it would lead to them thinking I was an accessory to murder. So I just lay in bed all day until I had to do my night shift at work. It had struck seven and my nightshift had just started. I was as a security guard at a museum. I was told I was working the 4th floor. I got in the elevator and got to the top. It was the slave trade floor and this made me feel even worse. Even though the trade is over, now there is still not equal rights. I was four hours in. It was now 11 o'clock. I was tired. I heard footsteps but I often did.

"My mind's playing tricks on me," I told myself. Two more hours in and I heard….

"Keith….. You could have saved me! But you left me to die."

What?

"Who is that? Where are you?" I shouted.

"I am nowhere any more. But I am everywhere," continued the voice.

I felt my heart beating so fast, like I had just eaten a foxglove leaf. My knees hitting each other as I shake. Then I saw it. Not like the movies. But a thing with a see-through white tint. Not a bed sheet over his head, but jagged clothes and then he growled,

"You could have stopped this!"

He glided towards me. I fell back into one of the exhibits and landed on a blade which slightly cut my calf. I ran, limping, then as I turned the corner, there it was! The monster glided through me like the scene in Harry Potter. I fell again, backward.

Beep! Beep! Beep!

I woke to find myself in hospital.

"Keith," the doctor said as he walked up to me.

"How do you feel?"

I said I was fine. The doctor preceded to tell me that I must have had a hallucination. I had a sigh of relief. I realised that the ghost must not have been real. The doctor told me to get some more rest. In the morning, I got out of the hospital. I didn't have my car, so I walked towards the bus stop. I saw the bus coming and started to run but I felt a sharp pain in my calf. I looked down and there was a cut on my calf! The memories came flooding back to me.

"So it was real!"

When I got home, I called the police and told them what I had seen. I told them that the black man had been killed by police. The officers where arrested and the burden of guilt was lifted off my chest.

THE BUTCHER'S SURPRISE

Dylan Jones

It was Christmas 2018. Mum dad and I had rented an old- really old cottage in Wales. It used to be a butchers shop, but now was a cosy, if not big, old and a bit damp smelling.

We were staying for five days, over Christmas to get away from everything.

The village was nice, it had a stream some nice café's two pubs a playground with large football field and a beach down the road. I even made a friend "Jude" on my first afternoon at the playground.

Jude was my age 11, he liked horses, and we played footy. We both support Liverpool!!

I asked him to come to our cottage for tea, and when I pointed the cottage out to him, he said, looking shocked, "not there are you??- that's the haunted house of the village."

He told me the story of the old butcher who had been killed there.   With his best butchers knife!

I thought he was being silly so we laughed and agreed to meet the next day to go and look at his horses.

After dinner, I sat up with mum and dad talking about Christmas, in front of the hot real log fire. Dad said "this lounge used to be an old shop", I asked "was it a butchers?" My mum and dad were amazed I knew so much.

I went to bed at 10 pm warm and happy having had some cookies and milk.

I woke up I do not know when.

The house was almost totally silent. Cold. The only sound was the wind outside and the creaking of the house's wooden floor, that groaned, as it got colder.

I could not sleep.

I used my torch to read my book, but I jumped as I heard a hoot from an owl outside.

I turned off my light and closed my eyes, praying for morning.

BANG.

Then there was a loud crash. I sat up with a start, called to my dad.

No answer.

I ran to their room, but it was empty. The curtains where blowing wildly.

Armed only with my torch I crept down stairs, squeak, squeak, squeak, all the way to the bottom.

The kitchen was lit up by the full moon shining in on to the kitchen top where the kitchen knives lay scattered out of their block, across the top!!!!

I turned to see the door to the old butchers shop (or lounge) was open, a sign hung over the door saying "Open for Business".

I screamed and ran up to bed.

I woke up at 7am, cold, clammy, tired. I quickly ran into my parents room and they were there asleep, I was relieved that it must have been just a bad dream.

I plodded down stairs, looking forward to my Crunchy Nut cornflakes. I got to the bottom step.

I looked up.

In horror I saw the kitchen knives scattered over the kitchen top, just as I had the night before…….

A Desolate Street

Sadie Cardall

I was walking down a desolate street. A street with ice etched into the pitch-black tarmac road. Nothing and no one could be seen. The only sign of life was my own breath hovering before my face, but it was barely visible as it merged into the fog that was lurking like a bad smell, and blocking the view of the surrounding houses and the direction I was to continue to walk in.

Don't panic. Stay calm. It's only dark and foggy. Nothing's here to scare you. These thoughts kept spinning round and round inside my head, but no matter how many times I listened to them, they never quite sunk in.

I knew this street; I've walked down it many times before but something seemed different. I wasn't sure whether it was the weather, but it had an *uneasy* feel about it. I continued with caution, looking at my feet so I was to not step on anything noticeable. Left, right, left, right, left, ri….. I suddenly dipped about a metre beneath the ground and murky lumpy liquid started crawling up my leg. I hadn't seen the hole that I had just fell into, it was so well disguised with the pavement I didn't see it. *Oh well, I'll just pull myself out.* I tried and I tried to get my leg out of the hole, but it wouldn't budge.

I started to feel a giant spider crawling up my leg, wait no, it was a hand. The hand was bony, dirty and had extremely long pointed nails that I could feel digging into my skin, desperate to hold on. I looked down to see what was pulling my leg, but there was nothing there. I jolted downwards into the hole by another inch, but there was still no hand or person there. *What was happening?? Was gravity changing right before my eyes??* My brain wondered off into thoughts of what the creature or force might be, but not for long.

The invisible hands grabbed my neck and every nail hammered into every vein and my windpipe started closing in and then… I couldn't breathe.

Come on Taome. You can do this. Just pull the hands off your neck. I tried and tried and struggled and struggled for at least a minute, but I couldn't get these glued hands off my neck. My vision started going blurry and I went dizzy, so dizzy that I felt like I was riding a thousand loop-de-loops on a rollercoaster. I passed out.

'Will she be okay, will she live?', I heard a shaky, panicky exasperated voice ask; a familiar voice. 'Yes, I can assure you that she will be perfectly fine, Mrs Oakley', this voice was one that I did not recognise, a soft, gentle voice. 'Do we know what attacked her?', My mum said, her voice was starting to relax into her normal self, though it was still concerned.

'Evidence proves that she was strangled, as there are nail marks on her neck. But we have no idea who or what attacked her as there was no one near her when it happened. We asked the neighbours if they saw anything, and they said they couldn't because it was so foggy'.

I opened my eyes and waited for my vision to focus. Once I could see clearly, I could see my mum sitting in a chair beside me and a nurse talking to her. They both looked at me when I opened my eyes and my mum stared at me for a minute, with a creepy smile on her face, then she came and hugged me. *This was weird. My mum never cared this much about me, it was her fault that I ended up like this. Well, probably, I couldn't remember what happened to me, but why?? And what was I supposed to do now? Why was mum acting so oddly? Perhaps I'm reading too much into it, maybe she's just being nice? But what if I am in danger, why don't I feel safe anymore?*

Then something happened that I least expected.

'Hello sweetheart, you're coming to live with us now, are you ready to go?'. There were two nurses standing in front of me. One was shorter than the other, with a blond bob and sticky-out ears. The other was taller and had a moustache with his hair tied back in a neat pony, it looked like he had a gallon of hair gel on his head though, I thought I could see my own reflection in it. However, the most striking thing about these people was that they were wearing enormous amounts of PPE, which I thought was unusual. *I didn't have a disease, what were they up to?*

The two nurses gave me no chance to move, think or speak and before I knew it they had yanked me out of the bed and were carrying me away, my mum waved, still with that creepy smile plastered onto her face. I screamed, and that was the last time I ever saw her.

A Horror Story

Alexander Clark

It is a beautiful day in Brazil. After a day's hard labour building houses we are walking back to camp through the dense, misty Amazon rainforest. As we are walking, I bend down to tie my shoelaces. I look up. No one is there. I call out. No answers. There is no sign of them. I am alone.

As darkness descends, a blanket of mist shrouds the forest floor in mystery. I can hear the birds calling, the frogs croaking, the chittering of monkeys the snakes hissing. I hear everything preparing for the night. I can barely see the cave at all, through the eerie fog. Even though it is night-time, the humidity is suffocating me. I don't know where to go. I am lost in this eerie forest. As I wander aimlessly, in some hope that I find my way back, I stumble across a cave. This would make a great shelter for the night. I hear a noise outside. A twig snapping. Branches crunching, snapping. I sprint inside.

But then, I feel a sharp pain in my calf. I hear a rip in my trousers. My leg is snagged on a rock. I feel the hot blood oozing down my leg. I fight not to scream, to shout. The pain is unbearable. I am in agony. Suddenly, I feel something on my ankle. It starts crawling up my leg. Then I feel another one, and another one, and another one. I reach for my torch, and I turn it on. And my worst fears are realized. They are giant tarantulas. And they are swarming all around me.

There are dozens of them. Crawling all over my arms, legs, chest and back. It is only a matter of time before the first one bites. Suddenly, I feel a sharp pain in my abdomen. The first bite of many. A few seconds of excruciating pain and then I feel another one in my groin. Another few seconds of agony. Then another one, and another one, and another. I try to tug myself out as an act of desperation. I know my attempt is futile. As, they bite more and more, I know my fate is sealed. I just shut my eyes and slip into darkness.

The Queen's Escape

Alastair Burgess

"Mum, do we *have* to move?"

It was Saturday afternoon, and Alice Tyler was about to move house, with her mum and dad. She had short black hair, black glasses, and pale blue eyes. She was short for her age, only 4ft 11, and she was 13 years old.

"Yes honey – we need a bigger house now that you're so tall," she replied.

"Yeah, imagine being *tall.*"

"Come on, we need to get going – it's a long way away." Dad said.

Four hours later, they were in London. Tall houses and giant flats and skyscrapers surrounded their small BMW, like an imposing army, decimating the nature that would have once had deer, boar, and sunshine. It now had pigeons that descended on scraps as if their life depended on it, the occasional cat, and grey, depressing clouds. It was too much for Alice, who had become so accustomed to the sleepy village of Almbrough, where the McDonald's seemed to hold half of the village at any one time that she found the idea that they would be living in London, very unsettling.

"I can't see any houses here."

And then she saw a giant castle, with grey bricks, four towers and a giant sign saying: "For sale". She started to laugh.

"How did you afford a dirty great castle?"

"Your father got it at a discount," mum said.

"And this is no ordinary castle, this is the tower of London," she said. Alice had heard about it at school.

"Isn't it supposed to be haunted?"

"You think?" Dad said.

"What? No!" Three hours later, Alice was sleeping in a bedroom on an airbed with stone brick walls and sash windows. Her dad had managed to modernize the house a bit, so they had sofas, a TV, an oven, and a fridge, as well as other things, but the house still had a sense of something unsettling to it. It could have just been the fact that so many people had died here, maybe in the spot where Alice was sleeping. The thought made her blood run cold.

And then she heard a noise. She remembered that ravens roosted on the battlements, but at the same time as the noise, an eerie light spilled through the keyhole. She sat up and turned her bedside lamp on. There was nothing in her bedroom. She creaked her door open.

She saw a sinister pearly-white figure in a magnificent dress, that was also white. Then she cried out as she saw the ghost of an axe fell on to the ghost of who Alice realized, was the ghost of Anne Boleyn, severing her neck.

The next morning, Alice told her story to mum and dad, who talked down her worries, saying they must have had a dream.

The family explored the house, and saw chandeliers, suits of armor, family crests, and empty cells which were around the size of a large kitchen table. They had barred windows, a bench, and grime down the stone bricks, that made up the room where countless men and women had wasted their lives.

The next night, Alice was ready, with a torch on, outside her bedroom with a torch on. Once again, the ghost went through the door. But Alice stopped her before she got to the spot where the axe would fall.

"Who are you?" Came the sound.

"Alice Tyler."

"I didn't know people live here." Her tone sounded cold.

"Well they do now. I *knew* it was haunted here!"

"Clever you. Aaargh!" Alice had shined the torch in her face.

"Get that off me!" She said. Alice moved it away.

"So how long have you lived here?"

"Ever since that wineskin Henry VIII had my head chopped off. He realized I was coming up to *Forty,* and tried to reject me, I *refused*, and he had my head lopped off. How did he die by the way? I hope painfully." She added.

"He died of natural causes and overeating." Alice replied. "So do you like it here?" She said.

"*Like it?* Every night I'm forced to walk here until that bloody great axe hits me. Would *you* like it?"

"I'm sorry. Alice said quickly, "Can I help?"

"You want to?"

"Well, yeah."

Anne smiled. Her cold tone seemed to vanish. "Well actually you could. Ghosts can't actually go through walls, but they can't open doors either. But you could open a door for me."

"Great," Alice said, "Come on then."

"Wait," She said sharply. "There's also a ghoul in this place.

Alice swore. "Where is it?"

They could hear stomping and groaning.

"Get in your room, quick!"

Alice sprinted back to her room.

The next morning, Alice's parents were worried. This was the second night in a row, and this time they had promised to wait for the ghost and the ghoul with her.

Anne Boleyn caused a commotion among Alice's parents, which woke up the ghoul. It came crashing through the door. It was at least 10ft tall, with gooey skin, muscly arms, claws and fangs. They shrieked. Alice picked up a sword from one of the suits of armor, her mum got a spear, and her dad took a shield. It moved closer. Mum lunged at the ghoul with her spear. The ghoul grabbed it, pulled it effortlessly out of mum's hands and crushed it into splinters. It swung its claws at dad, who blocked it with his shield, but was knocked to the ground and winded. His shield was snapped in half. Alice had sneaked around the monsters back and stabbed it, in the Achilles tendon, making it fall over. She then stabbed it in the head, killing it. They then led Anne Boleyn out of the door and watched her float into the night.

They had moved back to their house in Almbrough.

"Come on," dad said, "let's have a McDonald's."

Everything Went Black

Ellora Chatwin

Blood. Dripping down my hand, the blood of my best friend. What have I done?! A tall spider-like figure passes by, I follow it, forcing my feet and legs to take me to it. No hope, my efforts are futile, I cannot move. I am stuck here with my dead best friend, I lie on the floor beside him. His pool of blood staining my white shirt, regret and worry fills the room.

"What have I done? What have I done?!" I whisper, my breath heavy.

"More like what have I done," a creature whispered creepily, "You were like my puppet."

"So I didn't kill Arthur?" I ask, feeling a sense of relief.

"You did, but not intentionally!" The creature chuckles.

"So then how…"

"Close your eyes and it will all be over, I promise." The creature interrupts quietly.

I close my eyes, I feel someone breathing on me. The room suddenly grows cold, I trembled like the strings of a violin, something was touching me and I didn't like it. The claws of some kind of animal was scratching my neck, I could feel my fresh blood pouring down my neck. I was too scared to open my eyes, but maybe a peek wouldn't hurt?

I opened my eyes, not fully, but just enough so I could see what this animal was doing to me. Wait…it's not an animal! It's some kind of slit-mouth creature, with long sharp claws, the claws had dried blood on, a knife was drawn out from a pocket.

"All will be over soon!" It laughs loudly.

I scream.

"Don't worry, you won't feel a thing!"

It was then everything went black.

Him

James Turner

It started in London 1980. People going missing day after day. Most of them last seen at fashion shops or events. Everyone had no idea what was happening but one.

He would go into the streets of London with the night as his cloak prowling for his next victim. When He had chosen His next cog, He would stalk them from a distance like a lion hunting an antelope in tall grass until it was just Him and them. His steps were silenced by the wind as he approached from behind. His merciless knife plunged into the cog's head and he took the knife out it also took the life out with it.

However, that was not all for the victims. The cog was still to be put into the system. He took the body to a warehouse in the country side where his plans took place. He had a large container about two metres high and one metre long and what he did with it was far from natural.

When the body was dragged into the warehouse, he would first drain it of blood with methods unknown then the cog was lowered into the container full of this plastic-like liquid. A smile would show on his psychopathic face and, in his eyes, you could see the depths of hell welcoming Him. The cog was in the system. The body would be raised and the liquid freeze into the victim's skin. This yellow figure was His next mannequin to sell. He would go to the shops that he found the cog at and sell them as mannequins to the owners. The evidence is gone.

Will this secret ever leave a human's mouth or will it stay trapped in the jaws of Him?

Always Watching

Sophia Campbell

They say they are never really gone. They say they live on, their eyes lighting up the sky the way they used to light up your life. Their blurred features in the crevasses of clouds, their laughter in the gentle breeze that warms your face as you brave another day on earth; another day without them. Their voice concealed in the birdsong that fills the mellow sky of early morning with the melody of new life.

Others say they live on within you. They are a fire within you that never dies; a constant, eternal part of you. Until your fire is extinguished within someone else, and they are left to face the same unbearable emotion of grief that eats at you, piece by piece, day by day.

But, as I stood in the ice-cold church, the biting winter air snatching at my bones, the cold in my body jostling for the grief that lived in every speck of it, I didn't believe one word they said. There are only so many times the cyclical nature of existence can recycle you within someone else and I felt no inner flame warming my body that day. As the truth coiled itself around me, the blackness of reality strangling me, I felt no warmth within me, no loving eyes penetrate the ancient, arched ceiling of the chapel. Instead, I felt only the inconsolable emptiness that throbbed within the deepest depths of my fragmented soul. The pain that splintered within me, the anguish that took me away from my body until I was no longer the same living entity, but simply a shell for grief to inhabit.

A familiar black mist rose within me. It began at my gut, its billowing tendrils dramatically unfurling themselves around my spine, its hazy whisps stretching to every corner of my body as ice water fills a glass. Its blackness engulfed me as it continued to rise, before emerging in my throat, to choke me slowly, painfully with the charcoal depths of grief. The sensation triggered an inferno of pain that ripped through my body, a blazing fire of hurt piercing every cell even to the depths of my being. It filled my body with heat, a fire lit from the hearth of all I had been through, a fire that scorched my lungs and burnt my heart to a pile of ashes that fell, and landed, as softly as the sound of her whisper, at the very pit of my stomach.

It was an emotion I had never known before. Either it crashed through my body in sickening waves of hurt, or it remained as a numb ache in my chest; a constant reminder of all I had lost, of the demons that haunted me every minute of every day. The fog of grief that swallowed me before I had even opened my eyes each morning, and the knowledge, as clear as the midnight sky, that would I would never lay my eyes upon her again. Sobs escape my cracked and swollen lips, their overtones harmonising in the void of the cavernous ceiling, as the jarring dissonance of heartbreak echoes purposefully around the church. I splay my hands on the pew in front of me, my knuckles whitening as they grip the smooth mahogany, giving myself something to cling to, something to stop me from being swept away in the tidal wave of grief.

I attempt to summon any shreds of inner strength, yet they slip from my grasp. It seems that all that was strong and good and pure within me simply vanished the moment she did. Outside, rain begins to fall. Droplets pound the ceiling with the steady rhythm of life, a reminder that life goes on around my all-consuming vacuum of grief. They drown out the monotone voice of the preacher, resounding in my eardrums with an intensity that thrums within me, a tempo for my falling tears. We begin to head out of the church, my head bowed as I follow the stark rectangular box designed to house a whole person, a whole life, within four wooden slats. I walk towards a world truly devoid of her. A world never again privy to the most beautiful soul who ever roamed it.

The familiar black mist rises within me once more.

Some say I live on. Some say I watch the world from my vantage point in the sky, observing the leaves change from emerald to amber, seeing the oceans swell and grass grow and the sun rise every morning, its golden core spilling champagne out into the awaiting sky. Some say I live on within you. Some may even resign me to the dusty relics of history or banish me to the ever-expanding archives of time.

They say ghosts are meant for horror stories, only appearing when there is someone to scare. Only revealing their presence in times of trouble, waiting until the optimum moment to provoke the biggest reaction, the biggest fright.

Maybe that's true for some of us. But I'll always be here.

Always watching over you.

The Killer

Jack Hertzog-Garbett

Some call me Demented, I call me...

The Killer

'BAM'

I shoot the roof.

"Everybody down on the ground now! Where is he?" I shout in frustration.

"Where is who?" replies an innocent little child, bristling with fear.

"You know who I am talking about!"

I kick him across the room.

"Don't touch my son!"

The mum runs at me.

'SHING'

The knife glistened in the light and then it entered her body and I ground it about in there, it was satisfying, she was swept of her feet and fell to the floor dead.

"Anyone else want to test me? I asked a question and yet no one seems to have answered it yet. Where is he?"

"We don't know who you are after, please leave us alone" begs someone who clearly wants to die.

"Okay then I will go now then" I reply.

I walk towards the door and turn around and shoot:

'BAM, BAM, BAM, BAM, BAM'

They all fall to the floor dead.

I make my way back home; I have done enough killing for one day.

The Next Day

Beep. Beep. Beep. Beep. Stupid alarm clock.

Counselling. Why do I have to go to counselling?

Honk, Honk.

Hey, get out of my way.

It all slows down. This was inevitable. Everything I have done would have led me to this. There are only two ways to describe something like this: karma and inevitable.

The car flips over, and the windows shatter. The car enflames and is engulfed. I am stuck, I can't move. Oh yeah, it is just my seatbelt. I undo it. I smash the sunroof and climb out of it and stumble a couple of steps and then collapse on the floor on a heap. "I am awake, I am awake" I check my watch, I am half an hour late. "Damit!"

I limp the way to counselling.

"Jack, how on earth did you end up like this?" questions Bella the counsellor as I enter the room. " Well you see, when I was younger this man came charging into my house, I was only 12, there is nothing I can do about it, he asks me where my dad is, and all I do is say who are you? He grabs the top of my shirt and flings me across the room, I land in a heap. The man walks over and puts a gun to my head and says that he will only repeat this one more time, and he then repeats it and asks where my dad is. I tell him that he is upstairs in his office working, and he nods, he turns around and walks towards the stairs and I ask him why he wants my dad. He tells me he has been dealing drugs and came into his turf. I don't say anything I am too scared, and I am still trying to take this all in. The next thing I know he is upstairs.

'Bam, Bam".

I hear gunshots, and I hear the guy looking for me and then I can hear sirens and he made a run for it. I get out of the wardrobe and run upstairs, and my parents are both dead. He is going to pay for what he did.

"Oh, I meant why do you have blood all over you? "Enquires Bella. "Oh, I was just in a car crash" I responded.

"I Am going to go back home now I am really tired, bye." I continue.

Beep. Beep. Beep. Beep. Stupid alarm clock.

I grab the gun from my bedside table and shoot it, it is to annoying!

'Bam'

The alarm clock is absolutely obliviated. I hop in my new car which is brand new because when the car crash happened. I am a bit traumatised from the crash but, I just must look on the brightside of it. 1, I am not dead and, 2 I got a new car out of it which was well worth the pain. Killing is not the only thing that I do wrong though, I take drugs. The name of those drugs is called Cholesterol-lowering drugs, it can really affect you, which is what I am about to find out now. (Don't take drugs kids and stay in school.)

I take one of these drugs whilst I am driving and suddenly, I don't feel too good. I pull over the car as soon as I can, and I get out of this blasted car. I fall onto my knees (on the pavement) and start screaming "Help, help, someone call the doctor quick." The next thing I know, I am inside of this ambulance being taken to the hospital.

"Hey doc, is everything alright, what is wrong with me?" I ask the doctor.

"First of all, you need to slow down, second you will be going to prison as soon as you get out of this hospital and third you have had a massive overdose of Cholesterol-lowering drugs which has suicidal symptoms. You would have been getting headaches, feeling dizzy, feeling sick, feeling unusually tired or physically weak, digestive system problems, such as constipation, diarrhoea, indigestion or farting, muscle pain, sleep problems and low blood platelet count, it also makes you have memory loss. We have had a scan of your brain when you were asleep, and you have in fact suffered from all of these side effects. But there is one difference though. You didn't lose your memory, you rewrote it..."

You didn't lose your memory, you rewrote it" repeats the doctor. "Doc this is sure one hell of a lot to take in, I am going to go now and don't say anything, or I will shoot you in the face", I threaten. I walk out of the hospital and get in my car, I drive home. As soon as I get home, I have a pint of Guinness and try to think of what doc meant when he said that I didn't lose my memory I rewrote it. I spend the next 36 hours sitting at my desk rather having a pint of Guinness or thinking of what it could be, and then it all comes back to me. There was a wardrobe that I hid in, but it wasn't from the killer it was from the police. The day that my parents died I had found out that my dad was a drug dealer who had been going into other people's turf, and they were mad at my dad, but they never killed him…. I did. Because I was scared. But I can't figure out how my mum died. I spend another 2 hours thinking and then it comes back to me. She saw me kill him so then I panicked and killed her as well.

The killer was me.

Jack.

All along.

I walk outside.

Some call me Demented, I call me…

The Killer.

The Phantom Monster

Tara Odetoyinbo

When I was young, I always had haunted nightmares of this monster called the phantom monster, but this nightmare was different. It all started on a dark dreary night; I was at my dad's house and felt very upset. I couldn't be bothered. I had a feeling something was wrong. I didn't know why I was thinking that. What is going on? My Dad accidently dropped a plate. I went on a walk in the frosty winter's night, the breeze blew over my head which created nice sensation. I needed a break.

An hour later I returned home. I was angry, very angry! I was too angry to notice my dog lying dead on the floor. Pools of blood came gushing out of his eyes and head, it was like a crime scene. I did not know what was going on, my dad said nothing. I was upset so I went to my room. What is going on?

The next day when I came down and the same thing happened, my dad dropped the plate he was holding and the dog was lying dead on the floor ! What is going on? It's impossible. My brain was spinning, I was struggling to take in the recent events, I felt as if I had just got run over. My dad said nothing again. I wanted to run away from it all but I felt trapped. I felt like I was in a box, but it was slowly shrinking. I came to the sudden realisation that the Phantom monster is coming. I can feel it crawl up my back. Tugging at my hair. I screamed, no one heard me!

What was the point? I left the house chasing after something that I didn't know, something that I couldn't see. The Phantom monster is coming. Anxiety got the better of me. Phantom monster! Phantom monster! Phantom monster! The name was whispering louder and louder.

The Phantom monster is coming. What is going on? How is this possible? Too many questions! I can't think! Then I realised. But this can't be possible. Something must have gone wrong. Torrential rain came, more like a monsoon. But England doesn't suffer from monsoons. It soaked me but it burned, it burned very badly. The Phantom monster, I checked my pockets; I had my note pad and it turned out that I predicted this would happen. The Phantom monster is coming. I looked up and thought this would never happen, my world came crashing down on me like a land slide. There he was, the Phantom monster! My own Dad? The Phantom monster was standing in the distance, staring deep into my delusional thoughts with his demonic red eyes. A glare like no other. Its putrid, mouth was dripping blood. I knew I had to run, but I didn't. Why? I don't know why, The soul sucking demon came chasing after me. It came after its prey, I couldn't run fast enough. It caught up to me. It jumped on me pushing my face onto the cold wet rain. It scooped out my eyes out with its talons. It bit the back of my neck, I felt faint. My soul, it was taking my soul. I couldn't. When will it be over? That was it, I never woke up.

Oh No!

My world is coming to an end. Don't mess with the Phantom monster before it comes to get you.

The Nightmare Of Cinnamon Street, A Christmas Terror

Rishi Singh

December 24th 2015, 23:00. As moonlight fell on the city of Blackpool, the joy of Christmas seemed moments away but hell was awaiting. The people were waiting, for the presents under the tree but little did they know what was their Christmas present would be. 23:59, seconds from Christmas day. 00:00

, A gust of wind blew as midnight struck the sky went dark red as the world started spinning… the next time I woke up the lights were covered in spider webs the bed missing its legs my desk cracked in half, the windows shattered… the clock read: 24:01

I could barely feel my legs as I got up to look out the window. All of the windows of my neighbors were pitch black and the houses had blood splattered on them. I couldn't believe my eyes. This had to be some sort of sick nightmare. The next thing that came to mind was to go and check my parents' room. There it was both my parents on the floor surrounded with pools of blood. A shiver fell through my spine as I fell to the floor. As I looked up again a vase was shattered and the cupboards were open. The Christmas tree was gone… and in the place of the tree was a leaf less yew tree. Out of nowhere appeared a shadow *Christmas is no longer, for people around the world have ruined it with a lack of spirit.* That's when it hit me, Santa must be the one whispering this as I turned to look at the shadow, I didn't see Santa but I saw my grandfather. Not as a person though, as a ghost. The thing was that my grandfather had died years ago. He looked sorrowful as he stared deep into my eyes. He looked different; I didn't know why but I knew he did. His sorrow turned to and evil grin as the world began shaking. I lost my balance and fell to the ground… the last thing I saw was my parents lying dead on the floor.

Practice What You Preach

Prem Nagra

I turned into the graveyard, the keys to the tomb on my belt stiffened my stride, almost warning me to turn back. I sighed, said a prayer and unlocked the door. As I descended into the tomb, the decrepit door slammed shut. There was no way out. *It* knew I was here. I lit a candle for warmth and protection. Protection against the spiders, the dark and the monsters that lay within. I sank down further into the tomb. Each step coated with dust, my footsteps echoed in the darkness. *It* must have wanted me to suffer before I saw *It*, spiders crawled over every surface, including me. All eight of its legs, navigated up my spine to my neck; I waited for an inevitable bite but the insect crawled away, realising how weak I was. I finally reached the inner door, the gateway to Hell. I knew the inevitable was coming, I couldn't stop *It*; I stepped through the door to my fate…

I woke up from my dream, or should I say nightmare. I could not remember what it was about nor did I want to. I had more important things to do. Within an hour I was outside, the street was almost empty. I was one of the few (one of the lucky few) that were regarded weak enough to stay behind. My decaying leg would of made it near impossible to walk through the usual crowd on the way to the church, although I was still hindered by my stiff white collar. I had reached the graveyard, the words of comfort I usually give to the family of the deceased were meaningless. There was nothing I could say to comfort them, nothing I could say to comfort myself. There he rested, my brother right in front of me but a world away. Engraved on his coffin was: 1890 – 1942. After the service he was laid to rest in his tomb.

I unlocked the door to pay my final respects to my brother. Wanting him and me to be in peace. I descended the steps. It was unusually cold. I felt like I had been here before. It was absurd – I hadn't been here before… had I? Startlingly the inner door to his coffin was left ajar. I cautiously entered. I stayed there for only a few minutes reminiscing about my brother then, as I turned to leave, I hit the wood of the door. The door was locked. Suddenly, I heard the sound of wood moving behind me. Followed by a sharp bang that echoed in the tomb, made by the coffin door falling to the ground. I turned around and saw what was my brother.

He should of looked like my brother, but he didn't. He was similar in almost every way: his face, his hair and his clothes all perfectly matching who he was. But his eyes were lifeless and unlike my brother's. This monsters eyes, stared into the distance unmoving; though you were sure they were always watching you. As I saw this fiend rise from his coffin. I muttered half to myself "What in God's name are you?" My ears exploded with a deafening sound, a single message now lay within my brain.

"You dare ask what in God's name am I?" God does not exist. I alone am more powerful than your God!"

I opened my mouth to reply. But before my words of faith were spoken *It* interrupted.

"You have followed a faith blindly for many years, even bringing others to your path of 'holiness', but I will not be as heartless as to make you toil your life away for no reward."

As he said this, *It's* heartless eyes were now fixed on me. I was left to ponder *It's* words when *It* whispered to me.

"I will offer you absolute power for three days, absolute power to do fulfil any one desire you may have. After this I take you, I take your soul. Shake my hand and become this 'God' you believe in."

I sat there questioning my very reason for living and whether it was important enough to give up. Was this a folly designed to con me of life? Or was it a call to a higher purpose? A call to my destiny, to practice what I preach, to become God. Inevitably I shook *It's* hand. It immediately disappeared, along with my faith.

I woke up the next day, but this time the nightmare was real and vivid. I had made a mistake. There was no returning. My only hope of redemption to use these wishes for good. It was the only chance of saving my soul. At first my mind was empty but then the familiar news report came, with an update on the progress of World War 2. It gave me an idea. I thought about my wish and the room immediately turned cold, *It* was listening. I bent down onto my knees, closed my eyes and clasped my hands together, I wished for the war to end and once I had said that the ice-cold chill left the room, leaving me to wait for the next report of the war a few hours later. The next news report came: 'Allied forces have been overwhelmed by the might of the Germans, as we speak, France is being captured, there is nothing we can do to stop it, the war is over. Bombing planes are already positioned at England.' I was astounded by this, ironically the war was now over. I could almost feel *It* mocking me. I went through the rest of the day in a trance not focusing on my surroundings, only what would come tomorrow.

I had dreaded but anticipated this day, I was ready with what I wanted. The familiar icy chill came as I thought, "I want the Germans to stop terrorising us and other allied forces." I was confident this time that my wish was specific enough to not cause more pain and destruction. It took a few tense and tormented hours when the report came: 'Sources tell us that many important German military officers have fallen almost quartering their international power, scientists believe a highly contagious virus was spread throughout Germany due to this attack. The virus has also claimed the lives of many innocent Germans; surviving soldiers are retreating from allied countries. Though it might not be long until other countries fall to this virus.' I was distraught by this news, *It* had tricked me once again.

I knew what my final wish was going to be. The room turned sub-zero all the lights turned off and even the roaring fire place ceased. This time I spoke aloud: "I wish for my brother to come back to life." Unexpectedly the room did not return to its usual state. I realized now I had to go to where it all began and accept my fate. I turned into the graveyard, the keys to the tomb on my belt stiffened my stride, almost warning me to turn back. I sighed, said a prayer and unlocked the door. As I descended into the tomb, the decrepit door slammed shut. There was no way out. *It* knew I was here. I lit a candle for warmth and protection. Protection against the spiders, the dark and monsters that lay within. I sank down further into the tomb. Each step coated with dust, my footsteps echoed in the darkness. *It* must have wanted me to suffer before I saw *It*, spiders crawled over every surface, including me. All eight of its legs, navigated up my spine to my neck; I waited for an inevitable bite but the insect crawled away, realising how weak I was. I finally reached the inner door, the gateway to Hell. I knew the inevitable was coming, I couldn't stop *It*; I stepped through the door to my fate...

At first I was alone then my brother rose from his coffin, this time not possessed, my final wish had worked. My brother had returned to the world, or so I thought. "Where am I?" my brother said. I told him that he was safe, back home. At hearing my voice he was startled, he did not know who I was, or even who he was. I could tell that he would never be the same brother I once knew.

It had appeared once again, reassuming the body of my brother now with the same lifeless features. No words were spoken, I hung my head in shame as *It* dragged me to the depths of the underworld. All that was left in the tomb was the remnants of who I was, my cassock and white collar.

Hermione

Esme Mercer

An envelope addressed to me was sitting on the door mat when I went downstairs on a sunny Saturday morning in July. We had enjoyed just one week of our summer holiday.

I took the envelope to the breakfast table and opened it while eating my scrambled eggs. My parents were very intrigued as to what the envelope might contain. The only post I got was a birthday card each year from my Aunt.

The envelope was thick, the paper slightly scented and the handwritten text was exuberant. I carefully ripped along the top of the envelope and removed the paper within.

Its letter head was for a school... I had just finished prep school and was about to move into seniors. The letter wasn't from the school I was going to. "Wiltonian School for Girls" was in Oxford, a long way from our home on the Wirral. As I read further, I was invited to attend the school, based on my excellent performance in the 11plus exam, and my place would be fully funded as I would receive a scholarship for tutoring and full board.

My parents were as shocked as I was, and we all laughed about how ridiculous it would be for me to leave my family and live somewhere I hadn't ever been to without anyone I knew to be close to me.

Another week passed and a second letter arrived asking me to confirm my acceptance of the offer. My Father phoned the school and spoke to the headmistress who had written the second letter personally. It wasn't a hoax; the place and school were real. Over the week I have begun to imagine what it might be like to have a completely different life, an independent life, at a boarding school very like the ones in some of my favorite books.

On the train to Oxford, my parents with me, we talked about what I might expect living away from home, and I made my parents promise to take good care of my pets, my two dogs Binks and Rollo, my hamster Fluff, tortoise Voldemort and my enormous ginger cat Hermione. They would send me photographs of them each week.

The school was similar to my old one, a large open green space in the center with the buildings surrounding it. There was also a beautiful Chapel.

The first weeks were exciting, meeting lots of new people and making friends, and sometimes lonely as I missed my parents so much. Thankfully a lovely lady called Mrs. Beech looked after my dorm and became a close friend and ally.

The teachers were exciting, Mrs. Broom, our science teacher, was fascinating. Wearing black always, and heavy rimmed glasses, which made her eyes appear huge, she could be easily distracted and talk about ghosts. Sometimes her stories would make us terrified crossing the open green on our way back to our dorms.

One Sunday morning in early December the weather was foul, rain lashed down and the sky was near black, we were soaked wet through as we ran to chapel for morning hymns. Sitting at the organ playing was Father John, his thumping of the keys resonated around the stone interior. The light from the stained glass windows was dim, and the candles were not lit. The solitary light fitting over the alter was the only source of light. It was freezing, the grills running down the sides of the pews emitted not one breath of warmed air. We could see our plume of breath as we sang. It was so dismal that we girls started to gently giggle. Mrs. Marsh saw our shaking shoulders and a gentle low warning noise from her subdued our merriment.

It was during Father John's sermon that I heard the sound. It was a small scratching sound which seemed to come from behind me, I turned but couldn't see what was making the noise.

Toward the end of the sermon, I heard a very clear meow, a cat had most definitely made its way into the chapel to avoid the downpour outside.

At the end of the service, two hymns later, I turned to my friends and suggested we lag behind and see if we can find the cat. When they asked what cat I questioned their hearing, it was a loud and clear meow. I stayed behind and look under the pews, behind the alter and even in the organ loft.

Finding nothing I returned to my dorm. Mrs. Beech was waiting for me in my dorm. Jessica, who had become my closest friend was sitting on my bed, they both stared at me. Drawing me into her arms Mrs. Beech told me that my parents had phoned to let me know that Hermione has passed away quietly in her sleep the night before. My tears burned my eyes and it felt like I wouldn't ever be able to stop. Hermione had been my companion since I was two years old.

After lunch I returned to my dorm, my tummy rumbling as I hadn't been able to eat, I sat on my bed and looked through all the photographs my parents had sent me since I had left home three months ago. Tears returned to my eyes as I looked at Hermione in the photographs.

I spoke to my parents, and we all talked about the things she used to get up to. Hiding under the bed and attacking your ankles as you got up, jumping on the dogs as they slept, and her favorite trick of stealing meat balls off an unguarded dinner plate.

After an interesting week in school. On Monday morning Jessica swore she was being attacked as she got out of bed. Wednesday saw Bethany claim her meet balls had been stolen from her dinner plate. Friday night all the dorm were woken as some prankster leaped around from bed to bed.

On Saturday morning, I was talking to Mrs. Broom, and we were discussing the weeks events when a message arrived from my parents. They had sent a series of photographs of my pets. Voldemort refusing to eat his lettuce, Binks and Rollo chasing each other in the garden and fluffy asleep in her cage. We looked at the images together, I don't know who noticed it first, in the photograph of Voldemort there was most definitely a ginger paw playing with his lettuce. Binks and Rollo were chasing something, when I zoomed in, it was a ginger tail. The last photograph sent of Fluff was the final evidence, without doubt, the large ginger whiskered face that looked out from behind her was Hermione's.

The Ghost Hour

Kate Baker

A. and E. at 3am, is it the ghost hour? Sitting in the uncomfortable chairs, waiting, hearing the repetitive pulse of the machines. It's only us here...

The calling hour, 4:00am. It repeats in my head like footsteps when walking underneath an echoing bridge.

"Miss Mason" shouted the nurse. Walking through the big electric double doors, we take another seat. I have a gut feeling that something isn't right. What is it? Maybe I'm too tired, or maybe there is something behind me...

I can sense something.

When will the doctor come in? I'm so concentrated on this presence behind me but where is my ...daughter?

Blood rushes to my brain, I'm going to be sick. I stood up immediately with no hesitation ran back through the open electric doors. Shouting her name, "M...Matilda... Matilda... Matilda" struggling to get my words out.

,

A touch on my shoulder and I seem to wail, water streaming out of my open now red eyes. I know it is Matilda. I turn round with the biggest smile knowing we have to get out of here, my arms around this so like 'Matilda' figure. A skinny Matilda, a very skinny Matilda.

I open my eyes and it is what appears to me as a skeleton, brownish coloured hair shaped like an Afro. I repeat in my head, "a skeleton with brownish coloured hair shaped like an Afro?"

My arms now a defence barrier, just try and punch this so like corpse away from me. It is just me, running through these abandoned corridors. I pause for a second I can feel the sense again the same feeling I had when watching in the nurse's office. But this time when I turn around it is something unimaginable, something no mother would want to see…

The corpse, holding my fragile Matilda. The decaying skin, dripping off her face whilst being held up by this monster. All I could do is cry and run towards her, everything jumbling my mind. Why was her face decaying? Was it acid? Soon I realised it wasn't any of these things, but I wasn't sure. The bones where dropping on the tips of my toes a bone at a time. Soon there was nothing left of her. How could this have happened?

Annoyed, upset but my body just shut down like a like switch. One second, I was enjoying life. What do I do? I'm still stood in the middle of the hospital, nothing left nothing NOTHING… the monster disappeared it's just me.

Again, it's just me alone. Alone echos in my head for a while, the sound again the same sound and feeling terror. Is it the monster? I look behind and I see it but this time it's holding the decaying body of…

CRACKS

Han Khoo

Upon a deep dead hill, enclosed by smothering darkness, sat a house. The house groaned and swayed, tilting with the gentle winds which carried a lonesome scream. The single occupant of the house shivered in his metal room and curled up tighter. That was the first night I saw it.

It swirled and swooped like silver daggers flung about in some unearthly tempest. It twisted and clawed like some demonic caged creature. It killed and questioned and raged like an oncoming storm. It hunted, scanning the darkness to find me. And I, alone in the unknown of my homely place, I ran. I hid. I adapted.

I build barricades, and night by night, I reinforce them. I block the windows, and evening by evening, I strengthen them. I store food to last for weeks and bolt the door with an iron cast. As always, the creature is too late. Even tonight, like every night, it will fling itself against my fortress, hoping in desperation to find some crack that can force open my walls and crush my mind with an iron fist. Yet still my safehouse stands, and I remain strong.

It screams again. A howl full of pain, hunger and rage. It can't scare me now, I learnt to ignore it long ago. Or that's what I tell myself. In a few hours, I'll run out of food, and then I will be forced to brave opening the door.

Cautiously, I creep towards that thick mahogany door. My breathing, as always, is kept silent. Inch by inch the door grows closer. I gently reach out, my fingers brush the dusty handle. I pause. I can hear the creature tossing itself at the other side of the house. It won't notice my exit. I think. I hope. Heart pounding, I slide back the bolt then yank down and thrust open the door, as it slams behind me. I run, like prey from a predator, hoping to get away. Morning will bring safety and silence, so I need to return with my needs before nightfall. Before it returns to darkness.

Having stocked a bag full of food and medicine on my back, I slowly approach my house. At observing its undamaged condition I sigh, a great bout of relief releasing into the cool air. The creature must have given up once it realized I had escaped. Following the stone slabs up to the entrance, I enter, the lock clicks behind me. Glancing out the window, I see the village below me glittering like a diamond in fog.

Smiling, I climb the stairs, and unload my supplies. Checking that my room is safe, I step forward, a loud crack echoing through the silence. My foot goes through something brittle. Lowering my head, I behold the splintered remains of a rose-white bone crushed under my shoe. I stagger backwards, realization washing over me.

The lock on my door never worked, I had to bolt it over. And that window, I remember bricking it myself. How could I be so careless? Then, somewhere down the corridor, a creaking door swings open. I turn, sprinting down the stairs, which suddenly seem much longer than before. Tumbling from the last step, I brace myself, a sharp shooting pain travelling up my arm. Something sinister slowly slithers down the stairs, I can hear it. Deliberately, I pick myself up. Refusing to look back, I painstakingly limp along the dark hall. I finger the knife in my pocket, but I know, however good was, it's useless now.

Approaching the door, I shiver at the cool rancid breeze that tickles my neck. It's just in my mind. I can't hear it anymore; it must have gone. As my fingers rise and stroke the handle, silvery fingers rise and fall upon my shoulder. I dare not glance, an attempt to convince my mind of its illusiveness. I turn the handle down, but the door refuses to budge. After all these years, the lock finally works. A lock designed to keep the monster out, now keeps me in. And the keys are upstairs.

I barely hear the scream carried across gentle winds. My house groans and tilts slightly, enclosed by a smothering darkness. My house squeals, as if uttering a death cry. My fortress, that sits upon a deep dead hill, has a crack. A crack which I left open.

Stumbled

Rachel Hughes

I stumbled across a man; a man who had a mask of fear; it was too strong to see what was underneath. As the day was cursed with night, the stars occurred like glistening specks of hope, the lake was a deep shade of blue but did not have any signs of reflection or life.

This place is haunted, cursed, shadowed, and agonised with fear. There is a house just across the lake that is that is cloaked with decaying darkness. This house made no movement. It is like a snake, with two vibrant eyes at the front of the house and it sneaks up on its quivering pray with no sense of kindness. The man was a few metres away from me, but did not seem to notice me. He kept his eyes fixed on the house across the lake and did not seem to show any signs of hope.

With curiosity and desire I asked, "are you ok?"

I dreaded the answer.

"It's calling me," he said.

And he stumbled around the lake at a slow pace, stumbled with dread.

Canned Meat

Henry Worden-Roberts

Adam was regretting accepting the dare to go into the old meat factory. Everybody said it was cursed or haunted, and people saw lights on, and heard the machines working, as if it was in its prime. Adam didn't believe any of this. That's why he was dared to go and explore. It was deadly silent, as if someone had put a blanket over the whole factory, blocking out the noise of the busy motorway next door. His footsteps echoed around the vast machine hall, where meat was once packed and sent away to be sold. It was hard to imagine that this was once a bustling place, where many workers would work for long shifts. Now it was just a hollow shell. The machines loomed out of the sullen darkness and cast eerie shadows in the beam of his torch. It was cold in the factory. In fact, it was frigid, like you had just walked into a piece of the arctic. He headed to a door set into the far wall. He opened it, and walked down the stairs. As he was walking down, he could hear his shoes slap on the steps. They sounded wrong.

Warmth abruptly engulfed him as he descended. Adam was too relieved to notice the fact that an abandoned factory with no power couldn't be warm. Once at the bottom, Adam found himself in a large room with shelves along the walls. The shelves had cans of meat stacked on them.

"This must have been a storage room.." Adam muttered to himself. He walked through the room and noticed that the cans were not covered in dust and showed no sign of age, even though they had been sacked there for many years. Adam was puzzled. He also noticed from walking through, the rooms largeness mostly came from how long it was. He stopped, walking over to the cans on one wall. Each can had a name on it. Adam saw Eleanor Briggs, Jim Rickson, Henry Ankas, and many more. Adam felt a shiver going down his spine now. Cold sweat was running down his face. Further up the corridor like room, some cans were rolling on the floor. He hadn't knocked them over. Adam didn't want his name to be on a can. He didn't want to find out what happened to them. And then, something horrific leaned out of the shadows of the corridor ahead. Matted, black fur stained with meat and blood, a large mouth with razor teeth.

The creature grabbed him with one of its blood encrusted hands. It ran down the meat corridor to a machine. Adam was crying and desperately struggling, trying to get out of the things grasp. Adam was now falling, falling down a chute...

At the other end of the machine a can popped out. The creature picked it up and carefully placed it in a space on the shelves. This can read:

Adam Porter

Ghost Story: Corona Christmas - The Apocalypse

Murray Cowan

Friday, 13th, 2019

Cold was the night, when the wind whipped the very skin she stood in. As the cold seeped through to her bones, she heard footsteps in the bushes. Approaching Slowly. Silently. Spookily. She ran to the street, but nothing. She waited, and waited, but still… nothing! As she stood there, the cold seemed to strangle her. It slithered down her throat and choked her from the inside. As she stood there attentively, she felt an eery presence surrounding her. She stayed perfectly still. Her legs felt as though they were frozen in the snow. A cold breeze sent a shiver down her spine, and she felt an icy, raw touch on her. She looked round to see a mangled, undead face. Paralysed with fear, she stumbled back, a look of terror engraved upon her face.

Wednesday, 11th, 2019

Every house was lined with lights and filled with festive cheer. The town of Fernhill Heath was a pleasant one, nice people and area as well as plenty of SCARES!!

Every year on Friday 13th December, people dress up and make Christmas Spooky. Houses would change to a Ghoulish, Ghostly Spookmas. Everyone took it seriously, all except Jane. She was not a believer in the supernatural, she knew it to be a fake.

As she cycled along the road, the "Christmas" cheer was still fully underway. As she cycled on, she was filled with disappointment, Jane knew deep down that Christmas, this year was not likely to go ahead. Jane, also known as "Dr Jane O'Toole", is an epidemiologist at the Royal Worcester Hospital. Arriving at work, she swiftly changed into her scrubs and slalomed through the corridors of the crowded hospital, avoiding many obstacles in her way. She arrived at her viral lab, determined to complete her mission. She was the guiding hand in the vaccine department, of the hospital, she was in there day in, day out. Jane and her team of expert vaccinologists were testing and developing the correct mixture to defeat the abhorrent Covid-19.

The days flew by, and before they knew it, it was Friday 13th!!

Friday, 13th, 2019

Her team were becoming restless, they were getting nowhere; at this rate they were going to waste their lives waiting for the perfect concoction.

As Jane sat there, she contemplated the dramatic change that the vaccine development had on her.

As she thought and thought and thought, one of her colleagues approached her and said,

"Jane, Jane."

She looked up at him and replied, "y..ess, ah...yes?"

"We have done it Jane, we have actually done it!"

He was referring to the vaccine. They had developed a vaccine that worked on a cell of the coronavirus, killing it instantly. Jane brushed passed him and swiftly rushed over to the lab from her office.

But…on arriving she found the lab torn apart. At first, she thought it was a practical joke, but then she saw that the vaccine container was empty and there was green ooze all over the floor.

Out of the shadows came a deformed figure, its arms outstretched and its skin green and flaky.

"'BRAINS," it said in a grunt, "BRAINS!!"

She looked around and she saw the dead and decaying bodies of her lab team. Jane backed away slowly, the thing following in unison with her. Out of the corner of her eye, Jane saw more of these…things emerging from the condensing room.

What, there are more of them! What is going on! She thought to herself.

She Fled!

Jane was panicked now, her success was gone, her lab team were dead and she hadn't the slightest clue what had happened.

Out on the street chaos was unfolding, and there was mass hysteria. Jane looked back at the hospital and saw shattered windows, blood scraped walls and more of these "things" cascading down the building.

Jane rushed down the street terrified, confused… but then she saw him, a familiar figure, Steve, one of her colleagues from the lab. Amazed to see him, she approached…

"Steve, hello, Steve!"

"AH... Jane, it's you,"

"What is going on Steve, what happened in the lab and how are you still in one piece?" She asked in a rush, words tumbling from her.

"Well, not exactly one piece. The mutated creatures attacked me in the lab, in defence I put my hand out, but look". Steve held up his right hand to show his index and middle figure had been gnawed off. Steve explained.

"It was Graham! The senior technician, he purposely mutated the vaccine with a sample of lemon juice. However, he neglected to consider that it would corrode. It corroded his skin turning him into a deformity. All the others are dead, I escaped on pure dumb luck!"

"How do we stop them now?"

"There is no stopping them now! All we can do is wait for their race to die off and try to survive!"

Jane turned around, she saw people fleeing toward the woods and hiding inside allies.

"They're on a killing rampage!" said Steve.

"Steve, LOOK OUT!" shouted Jane!

Out of the corner of her eye Jane saw a zombie rapidly approaching them. Steve turned too late and was mauled to death by the savage beast.

"AAAAAHHHHHHH! STEVE!" Screamed Jane.

Steve's skull was now split open and from his decaying corps arose a mutated strain of Steve.

They began to peruse Jane. She ran and ran.

She stopped by a tree and rested. She was filled with grief and shock…and cold.

As the cold seeped through to her bones, she heard footsteps in the bushes. Approaching Slowly. Silently. Spookily. She ran to the street, but nothing. She waited, and waited, but still… nothing! As she stood there, the cold seemed to strangle her. It slithered down her throat and choked her from the inside. As she stood there attentively, she felt an eerie presence surrounding her. She stayed perfectly still. Her legs felt as though they were frozen in the snow. A cold breeze sent a shiver down her spine, and she felt an icy, raw touch on her.

She looked round to see a mangled, undead face. Paralysed with fear, she stumbled back, a look of terror engraved upon her face.

She was overcome by the creature, and torn limb from limb…

As she lay there, a look of HORROR… still etched upon her pale face!

I was Dared To

Em Keating

I was dared to go into the abandoned part of the school, in my school there are two halves of the once whole school, the 'new' school and the 'old' school, but over time everyone just forgot about the 'old' school, it was almost like it didn't exist.

Today I was sitting in the common room with my friends, Evie, and Autumn. Both of my friends are known for being daring, but me, I am quiet, reserved and sink into the background, so I never really get involved with their antics, until today. "Hey Hannah, I dare you to go into the old school!" they both said in unison, I stood there shocked at what they asked me to do, "I am no way going in there!" I said angrily, they should know already that they were overstepping my boundaries. They then said "have a little fun! It our last year at school, try to do something exciting!" this is where I make a big mistake, I said "fine!" Then the bell rang it was time for my first lesson of the day. Except that wasn't where I was going.

I ended up sprinting to the edge of the schoolgrounds and then I stopped in front of a huge building, this was it, the 'old' school.

It had a very dark and grimy exterior, all the windows were either smashed or blacked out, the walls were made up of rotting wood, this whole building looked very out of place, almost like a piece of hell came to the surface. I walked up to the door and pushed it open with little force and it slammed down onto the floor with great power, at this moment I now felt like someone, or something knew I was there.

The interior was uniform with the exterior, and from what I could see I was standing in a dark hallway with many doors.

My plan originally was to just run in and run out but, I didn't think it was that dangerous at the time, so my plans decided to change. My new plan was that I would take a peek into some of the rooms and see if they took my interest.

The first room I had had a peek into was and old girls' bathroom, it was disgusting, and smelled even worse than it looked. Despite my disgust I decided to look around the room to see what the source of this putrid smell was. I looked in one of the toilets and there it was, a great big pile of crap it even looked like it was rotting. Now that I looked, I decided to leave, as I felt as if I wasn't alone, I felt as if someone was watching me. I couldn't bare it any longer I wanted to leave this room. But suddenly I heard something, something that even to this day sends a shiver down my spine.

I heard a footstep.

I ran out of the toilets and into the hallway and there it was, I saw a figure forming in the darkness, a shadow stitching it self together limb by limb, it looked too unearthly to be real, It was something that is beyond human comprehension, something you should only see in your dreams or worst nightmare…

Was it a ghost?

I stood and just stared at it in disbelief I wanted to scream, I wanted to cry, I wanted to run but I couldn't, it felt like I was frozen in time watching as the seconds slipped away into the nothingness of what is the past. The ghost seemed to be a young boy with Victorian school clothing but it was all torn and filthy, his hair was dark and very unkempt he seemed to have been in quite the fight but the most haunting thing about him was his eyes they were like a knife piercing through me, he also stared back at me. I couldn't deal with it anymore, this fear of something so small, so I finally built up the courage and ran for my life , I ran straight for the door I didn't turn back I couldn't bare to.

After this my whole life went back to normal, I just went back to being a background character. But even now I can still feel something is watching me wherever I go, it almost seems to loom over my soul.

The Night That Never Happened

Rohan Kapoor

Lost, I was lost.

The trees had taken me hostage.

The woods.

My biggest fear.

The only glimpse of light was the gloomy moon that illuminated the floor of the forest. Shadows followed me everywhere in this eerie place. I could make out glistening mountains, painted with snow in the distance. The rustling of leaves and twigs followed my feet as though I was being chased. The tall, towering, trees watched from their height, looking down at you. I was being watched. My nerves were building up as I followed a winding path, near impossible to follow. The whispering of nature could be heard in every direction as I peered all around, scanning for danger. An unsettling noise floated throughout the forest. Nevertheless, I was alone. Alone and afraid.

I trudged along like a soldier, wondering if I could ever get back home. With every step, my anxiety increased. I was feeling more and more trepidatious at the thought of never getting out of here.

Hallucinations flooded my brain.

My thoughts disturbed my actions. I needed to face my nightmares if I wanted to survive in this isolated place. Redirecting my mind, my brain slowly began to cut out the apprehension and focus on what was important.

Resilience coursed through my mind.

I was now determined to find my way back. Now slowly walking with my head down I noticed that the path dissolved. I curiously looked up and saw a house. It looked ancient as I scouted it out. Its dereliction suggested it had been there for centuries as the roof had fallen in and the walls had deteriorated. Chasing green vines ran up on all four sides of the house. Haunted or not, I needed to find shelter, and this was the only haven in this desolate forest.

The battered metal gate creaked and with every step I got closer to the front door. The door rattled loudly like a vengeful python. The floorboards screamed under the pressure of my tired, wandering feet. The glistening spider webs decorated the interior. Whoever was here before me had good taste. The antique paintings shone like relics of old on the mantelpiece. An intruder abruptly invaded my vision. I thought my nerves tormented my eyes with mirages. Whatever it was, it went back to the shadows, leaving me anxious. A golden spiral staircase enticed me downstairs. I needed to find some warmth. I needed somewhere to rest, to regain my strength.

The tortuous windy stairs seemed to go on forever as I stumbled down them. Disoriented, I finally reached the conclusion of the tormentful passage. In front of me, there seemed to be an endless corridor, with hundreds of doors on either side. Trying each door, I soon realised they were all locked with heavy rusty barriers guarding them. To my relief, one of them finally opened.

Without second thought I rushed in, unsure and uncaring of the possible outcomes.

A putrid stench flooded my senses upon my entry. A crooked painting lay on the wall, gazing through me. A forgotten bed occupied the centre of the room.

Then I saw it.

A mangled corpse was lying on the floor. The realisation hit me that the scent that so overwhelmed me was rotten flesh. My feet took control, forcing me to marvel at it. There were two huge bite marks on the neck and bone blanketed the body. Before I could think about what had happened, I heard a thunderclap. As I peered in terror the carcass' head was facing the other way. Then right in front of me, the corpse stood up, dominating me, with maggoty flesh falling off it.

I froze. I stared into fear itself. The grim reaper peered back.

I blinked first.

Struck with horror, I scrambled as the skeleton advanced. As I cowered back, the corpse grabbed my face. Crushing my soul unconscious.

When I woke up, I was tied to a chair. Looking around the room, I saw the most uncanny and horrifying thing I have ever seen. There was more of them. Multiple of those living corpses were standing around me talking about their day.

'How was ye day Danny?' One of the corpses screamed

'Didn't get enough sleep, was a zombie all day to be honest Paul' replied Danny.

Paul noticed that I was awake and crowded around me, bloodthirsty. My palms started to sweat, the hairs on the back of my neck had stood up and my heart started pounding like a bass drum. My nerves were at their peak. I cowered in fear as their shadows grew closer.

They were right on me. Opening their mouths, I could see their black teeth getting ready to deliver a fatal bite. Suddenly they all went for me, biting and ripping my skin off my body with no precision whatsoever. I was in pieces, my skin everywhere. I became one of them now. I was no longer human, but somehow I was still alive. I could feel their savage bites as they were tearing me apart. This was a horror story, and I was living in it. I was stuck like this forever now, forced to roam and live forever as a rotten corpse. This is my story of how I became a living corpse.

'We caught another one!' said Paul.

Sorry, got to go.

Based on true events.

Watch Their Backs

H. G. White (deceased)

The body rots in the corner of the room, unnoticed by all who stand by. Their faces are engraved with worry as they converse over the plague, war, and death. They speak of other matters too: but those are irrelevant as the dead cannot hear the trifles of the living.

Her face is starting to decay. Little green lines crisscross over burst blood vessels, as purple shadows appear beneath her eyes. It was not an ordinary poison that took her. Navy and vermillion bloom around her neck – a necklace of bruises laced with spikes of red. Drool dried around the lips of her mouth, turning the pink flesh white with the dry, desiccated skin splitting open. Wind whistles through her hair, as it's now dull brown and flat but it was once glossy billowing like a pillow for her to lay her head upon before it slowly withers and ultimately leaves. Just like the others before it.

The girl's lips are slightly parted as vacant eyes stare up to the ceiling, her head lolling back. He was the first one to walk out, but the others soon followed. Like sheep to their Shepard. He's still nearby – he's one of the ones in the corner, with the worry lines etched into his face and drooping shoulders, as though he carries the weight of the world and its burdens. His back is to her. And now he's leaving again. He's walking through the door, coming out into an empty space, a dark atmosphere like that of a graveyard, except the landscape here lies still and unmarred by crumbled stone. Completely flat – everything totally desolated. As if a post – apocalyptic state has descended on the world, leaving nothing but the distinct figures of the people who move through the darkness. They're leaving the body behind. Better to leave it there to rot than to bring it with them and risk discovery.

She wears a bracelet on her upper arm, the sleeve of her dress falling away to reveal the darkened silver. The others wear it too. A symbol of friendship between the friendless, she was proud to be a part of the group. That was a long time ago. Now she dangles from the ceiling, coarse threads of rope entangling her neck, mixing with the violet bruises that now taint her the once pale complexion of her skin to form warped jewellery. Her arms sway listlessly by her sides, long pale fingers reaching out for them. The guilt overcame her forces. They all knew it would. In the end she was the only one who had a heart. And a mind that drove her to don a necklace of rope.

My body is covered in bruises and small cuts from running through the field of thorns. As the wind returns, it swings for a few moments, before gravity forces it stationery. I could stay here, watching as the flesh I lived in decays, fades away until nothing is left but the ivory pale bones picked clean by rats. Or I could follow them, watch another's life unfold where mine will not. I didn't plan to reduce myself to nothing but disembodied thoughts drifting through the atmosphere, and nor did I want to. We didn't learn much about ghosts when we were young, but there was always the warning leaning just outside our peripheral vision. *Don't leave the earth looking for revenge*, my grandma used to say, the thick smoke of her pipe turning the air foggy, *or you won't leave at all*. A cautionary tale. And if I am to become of it then become of it I will. I never did things by halves.

So, they should start to watch their backs.

Beating Ozymandias

Grace Klemperer

I went to Florida last summer. Commercial, alive Florida, where the flowers sing back - the Sunshine State. I went exploring a lot, trying to forget why I'd come away from the bustle of the city. I found strange things in the wilderness. Things that were purple, silent in character and not quite alive, but certainly not dead.

It was on my very last day in the Sunshine State that I encountered the amusement park - that long-forgotten merry-maker, seeping kenopsia through the cracks in the sand-roughened floorboards. The locals said children went missing there, or, at least, the local owls that roosted in the pine trees outside the wire mesh fence said that. But, after all my superstition, it's only a legend - one for the birds, so they say.

But the owls are watchers, too. Not fickle, these great and dignified fowls, and Athena chose well. Besides, they were there from the very beginning.

Two decades ago, a man named Ozymandias, a businessman, bought a plot of land in Florida - a forest where thrived wild roses and forget-me-nots and owls' nests - and he cut it all away and built an amusement park inside of a wire mesh fence. He advertised efficiently; posters depicted smiling, well-dressed families, who spent carefree afternoons exploring "Fortuna's Ferris," and "Thor's Hammer," and the carousel embellished with "The Owls of Athena." The drop tower loomed above it all, authoritarian yet enticing with the promise of a churning stomach and a fast-beating heart: "The Tower of Babel."

The amusement park made money fast. If safety checks were not always strictly enforced, and if the materials that formed the "Icarain Rollercoaster" were not carved of the finest of woods, it was only a minor issue, and not one that lost anybody any sleep. Least of all Ozymandias, who was making money, and was infiltrating the upper dregs of society. He was successful, powerful, and rich. King of Swings, he was known as. Men who had watched eagerly, anticipating the enterprise to wither on its first summer bough, looked on his success in despair.

Things changed when the First Lad got trapped. The owls never knew his name because no one ever came to look for him, but the owls were watching when he crawled into the cylindrical playhouse in the middle of the carousel. When the roof collapsed over him and the metal bar drove through his unhardened skull, the owls watched on, wise and helpless, their calls echoing his one, futile scream, cut short. They swore to remember him.

The amusement park lost popularity and closed down soon after that. Rumours spread, and were squashed. Ozymandias disappeared; some said he had moved to New England. But the owls saw him. They saw him slit his own throat, legs dangling over the edge of The Tower of Babel, and watch the blood flow down until it was all gone, and the owls saw him fall down after the red stream as though he wanted it back, wanted to drink it up again, and land with a soft thud and a biting crack on the dead, trodden dirt.

Weeks passed, and Ozymandias' body was found, and taken away by young men who worked for the government. Two generations of owls came and went, telling their tales to their children and the stars. The roses began, hesitantly, to creep back to their homes, and as they did a series of children began to appear. Young, bewildered, and seemingly only half-awake, they, time after time, would run from a breeze or a voice calling, "mine!" and drift brazen along the roller coaster tracks into the rising sea at high tide. Until quite recently, the owls had watched, and had listened, and had remembered, but they could do no more. Except for this: that they did, in their nightly songs, tell histories of the injustice that they have seen, in the hopes that, one day, on a charmed summers' evening when the roses had claimed Fortuna's Ferris for their own, someone would beat Ozymandias.

When I went to Florida in the summer, I met an owl named Aesop, who sang all this to me. I have noted it down for him, and also the tale that he related, which, though I cannot fully say I understood, I have felt a strange sort of duty to tell - this weird undoing I have encountered. The following is in the words of Aesop.

If you close your eyes for too long at the amusement park, trying to collect your wind-swept thoughts, you start to believe that your own, uneven breath is that of someone else, and you hear the wooden swings creak in the chill you hadn't noticed until now, and you catch the scent of the long-abandoned, and know that nothing here is known to anything there. Time has been forgotten here. You'll know that because you'll age a thousand years, and your hair and nails won't grow an inch, and your teeth won't fall out.

If you're not careful, you'll begin to hear voices amidst the other, more-or-less plausible sounds. You might hear laughter. It'll be hidden, yes, in the crackle and pop of the coke can you trod on, in the whisper and sigh of the vines you climbed to reach the top of the rickety ferris wheel, its ivy shackles long-since triumphant. But you'll know when you're not alone. If it's children you hear, especially because as you are one yourself, I wouldn't be too afraid. The children, for the most part, have been there for years; it's where they're safest. They only take the people who step on the forget-me-nots. You won't ever see them, though, because they're only phantoms now. But if you ever hear the man, Ozymandias – and you'll know who I mean because the wisps of time that were playing with your hair will stand still, and so will the swings at odd angles – if you ever feel Him shudder through your brittle bones... You should try to run. Not away, you'll never make it, but if you can get to the middle of the carousel where the First Lad got trapped all those years ago, you should be safe.

And when you hear His silent, deafening laughter die away, and you take your hands away from your ears and eyes and feel ashamed because you are sad to be alone again, and wipe away the blood on your face that came from one of your knees, you'll be able to stand, shaking, and crawl out from the carousel to realise that the sky got darker, and you can wonder if They - The Family - the one that gave you food and clothes and not a scrap of affection - will even notice that you're gone. And you can begin to climb up the wild, white, rose vines that conquered the peeling, rickety, wooden roller-coaster on a charmed summer's evening long ago. You'll probably cut your hands on thorns and nails and splinters, but you probably won't mind because the moon looks safe when it's so close.

And, if you don't put your whole weight in the rotten scaffold, and your arms aren't shaking so much that you can't pull your tiny form up to change to shadow far below for the first time since the last time a lost soul was here, you'll notice that the tracks go on and on down the sand dunes until they are claimed by the sea. And, because, at this point, you won't be thinking straight, you'll start to walk along the tracks with your arms stretched wide even though you can't fly, or, at least, you've never tried before. You'll reach the edge if you don't fall through any planks, and you'll stare down at the waves and know that the time for running was years ago. And you'll be lonely; so, so lonely, and you'll see the mangata, and the waves' whispers will be the children placing bets on whether you'll take the final step.

And you will, of course you will. You always knew you would. And the sea will at once sting and caress you, but you're used to that, aren't you? And you won't fight it, because the darker it gets, the better you can hear the children, and they say kind things about your hair-slides. You'll smile then, as the water turns to ink and clogs your throat and stains your teeth blue, because you drew a flower in the dirt with the heel of your dirty, yellow converse while you were crouched in the middle of the carousel where the First Lad got trapped all those years ago, and Ozymandias can't get in there anymore because the children keep Him out. The middle of the carousel, the sacred place, the hallowed ground. But life and art and beauty, beauty in the simplicity of a child's drawing, those things will last. And the flower will spread its spell, and now when lost children are lured, blurry-eyed, to the amusement park they will find comfort, not The Terror.

That means that you reclaimed it. You *beat* Ozymandias.

And if no one else, the owls will remember your sacrifice.

PLAY WITH ME

Ramsey Campbell

When Jackie lurched awake, the only sounds were the whisper of the sea a quarter of a mile away across the beach and the shouts of other people's children. She was afraid she was alone until she twisted onto her back. Her five-year-old son was almost within reach, using a stick to sketch somebody half buried in the sand. "Don't bury me, Tom," she said.

"I won't if you'll play catch with me."

The thought of a ball game made her feel more tired than ever. "I will soon, all right? Just let me have a little nap."

"There won't be time." As if he didn't want her to overhear his disloyalty Tom mumbled "Dad would."

His father might have if it was too early to get drunk and knock her about, Jackie refrained from saying. Driving halfway across England had felt even more like escaping from him than her divorce had, but it had exhausted her as well. She'd wanted to give Tom a few hours on the beach once she'd unpacked at the hotel. The sun was above them, casting the shadow of a root that groped out of the edge of the cliff near the top of a zigzag path. "We'll have time for a game, I promise," she said. "Be a good boy and give me half an hour."

"I won't know when that is."

"I will," Jackie said, setting her phone alarm. "Don't go far away," she told him and was inspired by her silhouette, pointing like the indication of a sundial at the cliff. "Stay by my shadow."

"All right," Tom said, though not as if it was. She held his gaze to make certain he knew she was serious as she sank down on the sandy blanket. Then her weighty eyelids intervened, and she was asleep.

"Play with me."

The plea didn't quite waken her, not least because it was hardly so much as a whisper. "No alarm yet," she protested, possibly aloud. She clung to sleep even when disintegrating fingers found her face, since they had to be sand carried on a wind. She didn't waken until a shiver travelled the whole length of her. She blinked and saw the sun lowering itself towards the sea. It was close to setting, and she'd slept through the alarm.

Tom must have taken pity on her and let her sleep. She was thinking how to make up for his lost game as she turned over. He wasn't behind her. All the families she'd seen earlier had gone, and she was alone on the beach.

As she struggled to sit up she saw two things that disturbed her more than she understood. The lopsided rickety figure Tom had drawn, which might have been composed of little more than sticks, could just as well have been climbing out of the ground as undergoing a playful burial. And the descending sun had extended her shadow all the way to the cliff. She took a breath so fierce it gritted sand between her teeth and cried "Tom."

Her voice sounded small as a child's under the dimming sky. It was the solitary sound on the beach, where the waves were more distant than ever. Surely they were too gentle to have carried Tom away, and besides, she was all too sure that he'd followed her shadow to the cliff. While she was sleeping the shadow might have led straight to the path, and he could have taken that as an excuse to climb up just a little way, just a little further since she was asleep, just to the top... Surely he was up there and unable to hear her, even when she called with all her voice, and she ran to the path.

It turned back on itself several times on its way up the cliff. As it made her dodge back and forth Jackie felt she was trying to lift the sun above the horizon. The sun rose with her, though not very far. At each bend in the path she shouted Tom's name, which the sky seemed to shrink even smaller. She was nearly at the top when she caught sight of a mass of rubble almost hidden by overgrown earth on the side of the cliff. A building must have collapsed down the cliff quite some time ago. It distracted her from an impression that something wasn't on the cliff that ought to be. She couldn't bother about that now. She had to find Tom.

As she strode up the final stretch of path she was preparing to tell him to come here at once, but the words expired in her mouth. Over the edge of the cliff she saw flat land miles wide, and it was utterly deserted. There wasn't even a hedge Tom could be hiding behind. Jackie stumbled onto the cliff top, desperate to think the grass was long enough to hide him, but even standing shakily on tiptoe only showed her how alone she was except for her outstretched shadow. She could see more of the beach now—the emptiness of the beach. She cried Tom's name a last time as she snatched out her phone to call the police.

"My son's lost. I've lost my son. He's five. I'm up on the cliff above the beach and I can't see him anywhere. I'm by the building that fell down the cliff."

"The old church."

Presumably it must be. She had to give her name and Tom's and other information that felt as though it was holding up any help. Long before she was assured the police were on their way, she wanted to ring off. She pocketed the phone and saw her shadow imitate her, and at once she knew what she'd missed seeing as she climbed the cliff: the shadow of the root just below the edge. What could the root belong to when there was no vegetation up here except grass? The question seemed worse than trivial while she didn't know where Tom was, but perhaps she needed some distraction from her fears, and she made for the edge of the cliff. She hadn't reached it when she saw she was walking on a pavement almost hidden by grass.

No, not a pavement—a crowd of stone slabs. When she stooped she made out words and numbers carved on the nearest slab—a name and dates, almost erased by moss and weather. More than that was written on the slab just above the hole in the cliff where she'd seen the protruding root. The letters and digits looked etched by shadow. She hadn't time to read the name, because she'd seen the dates and the inscription beneath them.

1871-1876. HE NEVER PLAYED AS A CHILD SHOULD.

Did this mean the child hadn't had enough of a chance, or that he'd played unlike a child? He'd been Tom's age, and now Jackie remembered the plea she'd heard in her sleep: "Play with me." The whisper had been so thin it had scarcely sounded like a voice—not Tom's, at any rate. In panic and confusion she ventured to the crumbling edge of the slab and leaned over. Not just the shadow of the root was missing. The twisted root was gone, and now she realised how much it had looked like a shrivelled arm reaching out a small hand robbed of flesh.

She was afraid to go closer, but she had to see. Dashing down the path, she activated the flashlight on her phone as she came to the hole in the side of the cliff. It was a few feet lower than the slab and almost level with her face. When she shone the beam into the hole she saw it was blocked by a rubbery object bearing ridges caked with sand—the sole of a shoe.

Earth gathered under her fingernails as she groped to drag the shoe out. Yes, it was Tom's, with the frayed lace she'd meant to renew tomorrow. He must have put his shoes back on to climb the cliff. Now that the hole was clear, she could see as far as a bend, where the tunnel led upwards. There was nothing like enough space to let her follow. With her free hand she began frantically to dig earth out of the hole to widen it, and was almost too afraid to call Tom's name.

It brought an instant response—earth spilling into the bend from above, and a sound of rapid slithering. She couldn't help recoiling, and grabbed at the hole to save herself from backing over the edge of the path. The phone flew out of her hand to skitter down the cliff. The sun had sunk unnoticed, darkening the world, and so she never saw the small hand that seized hers. Surely Tom's couldn't have already grown so thin.

'Play With Me' copyright Ramsey Campbell

Lightning Source UK Ltd.
Milton Keynes UK
UKHW050642060223
416538UK00010B/637